LOUISIANA BOUND II
The Mystery Continues

DONNA HANKINS

ISBN: 978-0-578-73914-4
Edited by: Todd Barselow
Cover by: Suzie Albracht

LCG
Louisiana Cajun Girl

DEDICATION

To my awesome children, Denise, Michael, and Laura, who has always been there for me.

Also, to a special couple, Uncle Simon and Aunt Louise, who has always been the glue that holds our distant family together.

Here is a mighty shout out to my loyal fans that encourage me with your enthusiasm and joy of my work. It's because of you I keep writing.

Contents

CHAPTER 1

The sun was bright and reflected mirror-like off the bayou, blinding me and taking me back to the life I had several months ago. The life I had led and loved in New York still sat like a boulder on my chest. Once, I was on top of the world with everything and anything money could buy. I had loyal friends, an impressive job, and a hard-working husband. Day by day, that charmed life slipped through my fingers and disappeared into nothing. The life I once trusted in, depended on, dissolved. The people I thought were my friends were not; the husband I thought was faithful was not. The job I thought would be there forever was not. The city I thought would be my forever home was not. Even the Church I went to, that I thought was close to God, was not. How could I have been so deceived? Everything I put my trust in was pulled out from under me like a rug.

By a divine miracle from God's Angels, I was shown a new life in Louisiana, a place I wasn't even sure was on the map, to live with people I thought were beneath me. To live in the worst place imaginable with dangers by every tree. But as the days progressed, a new life was formed, a life of unending possibilities. The people were genuine, good-hearted, and down to earth; unlike any people I had ever met. I found true friendship, the kind of friendship where people cared about you for who you are and not what you have or what you could do for them.

With a glance at Jessie, my heart burst with overflowing emotions, causing me to smile at the pleasant warmth spreading across my chest. I even found love in Louisiana. Love from a man who wanted nothing from me but to be loved, a man that would lay down his life for me.

In time, when the blinders fell from my eyes, I found a true beauty like no other place I have ever seen. In Louisiana, I found miracles, a sense of love and peace that only nature can provide, a place where nature had made its own tapestry of beauty that even the most talented artists couldn't recreate.

Above all else, I found God. A God that I thought was about money was not. To find out that God was all about love, and acceptance, and was genuinely real, as tangible as the sun on my face and the wind in my hair.

My heart overflowed with thanksgiving. I thank you, God, for showing me a life that is not built upon money or any material possessions but on love. And most of all, I thank you God for accepting me, me, Sarah Hamilton. Not for what I do, or own, but just because I'm here.

I owe thanks to Jessie too, as he showed me so much truth. The truth of a God that even nature bows down to, a God who makes the sun and moon shine on me just because he loves me. Everything in nature gives off vibration from the Creator and has a purpose, just like the workings of a clock. Because of this new God, I found that my life has more meaning. I can feel His love from the people around me and even in the waters of the swamps.

It jolted me back to reality when the boat hit the dock with a thud, the same dock that Jessie put back to its original order. My eyes gazed up at the house which had been in shambles when I moved in, but now looks like a picture in Home and Gardens. Jessie has done so much for me since I moved in. He's been there through the rough times with the break-ins and Hank's mental breakdown. I'll sure be glad when my divorce is finalized and my new life with Jessie takes off.

After a wonderful night at Jessie's house, I was eager to get back home to finally get the hall closet in order. I was eager but frustrated since I hadn't been able to achieve my goal of cleaning up the living room and reorganizing that darn closet, which took every spare waking moment in my mind. I couldn't help wondering about the reason behind a closet that had a mind of its own and continually opened and had water appear and disappear in front of it. The mystery of the hall closet needed to be solved. And if it's the last thing I do, I will get to the bottom of it.

It was close to one in the afternoon and the heat was so miserable that my shirt was damp by the time we made it back. Jessie was still pale as he recovered from re-injuring his gunshot wound and the subsequent infection. Thanks to that gun-happy, almost ex-husband of mine who had the nerve to think there was buried treasure in this old house from the eighteen-hundreds. I knew Hank was money-hungry, but his obsession with the theory was ridiculous.

The trip to Jessie's house yesterday sure took a toll on him. It was the first time we had ever spent the night there. He was just too drained to make it back to my house. Jessie was not bouncing back as quickly as I had hoped. My goal once we docked the boat was to get him in the house and settled.

"You're still looking pale from last night. I think you need to go lay down for a while," I said, worried about him and needing a good excuse to get back to the disaster in the living room.

Jessie's hand lifted my chin to look at him. "You will make a great mom one day."

The shock hit me like running into a brick wall. "A mom?"

"Yeah. You want kids one day, don't you?" Jessie asked with a hopeful look on his face.

"I've never really given it much thought. You know, I came from a self-absorbed world in New York. Thinking about anyone else other than me just didn't happen often. So I've never really considered it. But I have to admit, the thought of having kids with you sounds nice."

Jessie smiled, "That's my girl." He kissed my lips gently, then walked to the bedroom to rest.

The air was knocked out of me, but in a good way. Kids had never fit into my plan before, but my heart flooded with warmth as I thought of having children with Jessie. A part of him and I all wound up in one little person to love. Oh wow, that would be great.

Once I was sure Jessie was resting comfortably in bed, I closed the bedroom door hoping not to disturb him. I walked to the living room and stood there looking at the mess with my hands on my hips. "Well, it's finally time to tackle this disaster." I declared to the world. I would achieve my goal today come hell or high water.

Since I had already gotten rid of a lot of unnecessary junk, my only decision was where to put the clothes and boxes that were left, so I could finally reclaim my living room.

I felt relief knowing my OCD would be fed today. All I wanted was a clean, well-organized living room and closet. I looked from the mess on the floor to the tiny closet and still wondered how it would all fit.

I walked over and eyed the closet to find Aunt Pauline's dress on the floor. It was so heavy that the flimsy wire hanger had bent, letting it slide down into a heap.

I found an old wooden hanger to use for the dress. "That should hold you." Contemplating each garment, I slid one piece of clothing at a time to make sure I still wanted to keep it.

Aunt Pauline's blue dress was a definite keeper, only because of its uniqueness and how long Jessie said she worked on it. There were a couple of coats, a gray sweater, and a long robe that I kept.

Since the closet was dark and the string to the light bulb was short, I retrieved a chair from the kitchen and placed it almost under the shelf so I could climb up on top and examine the string, which looked cut.

"Well, this just won't do," I said aloud to myself.

I climbed down from the chair and headed to the kitchen to find string and scissors. Since I knew this would be a long and tiresome task, I made coffee. The fresh, powerful aroma of the local coffee smelt so good that I poured myself a mugful instead of one of the smaller cups Aunt Pauline had. With string, scissors, and my coffee in hand, I peeked in on Jessie.

I smiled when I saw he was napping. I was so thankful Jessie was obeying the doctor's orders this time and getting all the rest he needed, but I also knew the trip across the bayou to his house weakened him and he probably needed the extra rest.

I made my way back to the closet and stood on top of the chair, placing my coffee, scissors, and string on the shelf within easy reach.

After steadying myself on the chair, I cut just enough string to fall past the shelf so I could reach it readily from the floor. Struggling to keep my balance and tie the new string to the old string, I accidentally hit and knocked my coffee mug off the shelf, which hit the floor with enough force to shatter into pieces. I jumped down, careful to avoid the shards of the now-demolished mug, and ran back to the kitchen for paper towels. On the way back, I peeked in on Jessie again to make sure I hadn't awakened him. He was still out like a light, thankfully.

I gingerly picked up all the pieces of the shattered mug, then kneeled down to wipe the coffee from the floor. But there was very little left. It looked as if most of the liquid had slipped between the floorboards of the closet.

The wood that the floor was comprised of seemed different from the wood elsewhere in the house or in the other closets. As I examined it closely, I noticed that the wooden slats were spaced wider apart. It was the same cypress, but there was a coarser feel to it as if it hadn't been sanded well.

I could hear a drip, drip sound, like water hitting water. I leaned closer to the floor to listen and realized the dripping was definitely coming from under the floor. How could there be water under the house when it hadn't rained in weeks?

I went back to the kitchen to look for a flathead screwdriver, but only found a butter knife handy. Since my OCD would not let me walk away with coffee in the cracks of the floor, I was compelled to wrap a paper towel around the flat butter knife to clean between the slats.

Surprisingly, the wood shifted as soon as I inserted the knife. How strange that they didn't have the floor nailed down properly.

Then it hit me. Could this be another hidden passage? I wondered.

Maybe that crooked lawyer, Brian Thibodaux, lied to me and there was a cellar in this house. It sure wouldn't have been the first time he deceived me.

I pulled and tugged upon the wood, producing a panel of six slats of cedar nailed together at the bottom of the closet's floor. I lifted the panel and peered down into the unlit hole, hoping to see under the house. However, it was so dark I couldn't see anything. Since this was a pier and beam house I knew the sun should be streaming underneath the house, even though it was late afternoon, but all I saw was darkness.

I grabbed the flashlight and investigated further. Holding the panel up against the back of the closet wall, I looked into the hole until my eyes adjusted to the gloominess to find a wooden ladder to the right. My eyes scanned down the ladder until it disappeared into the darkness. As I positioned myself further hanging down in the hole in the closet floor, I discerned that the darkness was not a floor, but standing water.

I wondered if I should wake Jessie to show him what I found. No, I'll just take a quick look and I'll be right back. Besides, he needs to rest, I told myself.

As I contemplated my next move I remembered a pair of black rubber boots on the floor of the kitchen pantry.

The thrill of a new discovery had me tearing the kitchen pantry apart trying to find the rubber boots.

"Where did I see them old boots?" I whispered to myself. "There they are." Excited, I sat at the kitchen table putting on the black rubber boots. I looked down and smiled. Me, in rubber boots... what a hoot. To be on the safe side, I dug in the utensil drawer and grabbed a long, sharp knife. You never know... you might need a little edge to defend yourself from something in the dark down there, I thought.

Armed with a flashlight in one hand and knife in the other, I took a deep breath and started down what looked like a never-ending ladder into inky blackness.

I could hardly grasp the stairs; my hands were shaking so badly. Something was wrong. The excitement I'd initially felt faded and I could feel dread welling up from deep down inside. I paused for a moment, wondering if maybe I should wait for Jessie to wake from his nap.

No, I need to do this myself. I can do this, right? I'm only going to look around. No big deal, I coached myself.

Holding on for dear life, I cautiously made my descent into the darkness below. When my foot hit the wet floor, I could feel the cold compression of water around my ankle through the boot and was thankful the water didn't go over the top. It was close, but I was safe from getting wet.

It was dark and dank, and the odor was nauseating. It reminded me of the smell in Aunt Pauline's refrigerator before I cleaned it out. A combination of mold and spoiled rotten meat rolled up into one horrific stench. I wondered if maybe the sweet-smelling cedar in the closet had kept the awful smell from seeping into the hallway.

Since the water was fairly deep, I decided to only pivot to the right a little; afraid the water would spill over into my boots.

I see now why they don't have cellars in the south; I thought to myself.

My eyes scanned the room along the walls, finding that the space was just barely bigger than my bathroom. I was surprised to see that they'd made the walls of long strips of old wood. As the light shone brightly from the flashlight, my gaze hit some shelving with mason jars of food against one wall.

As I turned to leave, something caught my eye in the far corner. Dread filled my mind like an evil shadow of doom. My hands shook uncontrollably as I slowly raised my flashlight to see something or someone sitting in an old wooden chair in the corner.

My God, it was hideous. The scream pierced the darkness, and it took a moment before I realized it was me who was screaming at the top of my lungs at the horrible sight before me.

I couldn't move. The shock and fear that welled up inside me made my feet and legs heavy as if I was weighted down by cinder blocks.

The room spun around and around, causing me to drop my flashlight to grab the ladder tighter to keep from falling. I looked down at a small glow of light from the immersed flashlight below the water level, which made everything seem eerie and scared me even more.

With my back to the grotesque figure in the corner and no flashlight, I hugged the ladder to my chest as I hyperventilated to the point of nearly losing consciousness. Terrible images were flooding my head of a boney hand reaching out from a decaying zombie and grabbing me from behind.

I couldn't run or climb the stairs—all I could do was scream.

I lost all sense of time and didn't realize Jessie was trying to get me up the ladder. All I knew is that I wasn't about to let go of the ladder that held me upright and kept me from falling into the abyss of unconsciousness. That ladder was my lifeline. It was a way of escape if only I could move.

My mind raced as I imagined every possible tragedy that could lurk in the cellar. Five o'clock news reports: "Young woman found dead due to a zombie attack in her basement." Or better yet: "Unsuspecting woman was eaten by alligator found in a basement full of water." I didn't know what else could be lurking behind me and didn't want to know.

In my reality, I let out one long petrified wail, but Jessie told me later that it was one scream after another.

Jessie struggled to pull my arms from around the ladder. I couldn't and wouldn't budge.

Then I felt a sting across my face. I gasped and realized Jessie was there, and fear was replaced by anger. He'd slapped me across my face. How dare he.

Then I realized he was trying to help me, and I finally obliged him as tears ran down my face.

Jessie pulled me out the hole and forced me to sit in Old Blue, my trusted recliner since my college days, and my main comfort for many years.

"Stay here," Jessie yelled at me several times.

I couldn't let go of his hand, shaking my head no as he tried desperately to release my grip.

"It will be okay. Stay here where it's safe."

"Safe," I whispered weakly and let go of Jessie.

I watched as he climbed down into the hole in the closet floor, waiting and holding my breath. What if he doesn't come back? What if the zombie or an alligator eats him?

All I could do staring into space was hug myself as I tried to keep my body from vibrating me out of the chair. I crossed my arms around myself tighter to try to control my shakes, to no avail.

Jessie's head popped up from the closet floor, causing me to jump in my chair. He was holding my flashlight and immediately ran to the phone.

"Gerald, this is Jessie. You need to get to Sarah's house immediately. We found a dead body."

CHAPTER 2

The front yard of my house was lit up like a typical New York City night, as one vehicle after another materialized in the front yard. We had First Responders along with the Fire Department, Paramedics, Coroner, Sherriff's Department, and two men working on pumping out the water in the basement. Outside the driveway were some bystanders, possibly neighbors that were probably thrill-seekers following what little stir of activity there was in this part of the country, just standing around watching and waiting to see what all the commotion was about.

It's not every day one finds a dead body in the basement of a house that's not supposed to even have a basement. With finding six to nine inches or more of water down there, I could understand why people in this area didn't have basements and why the dead were buried above ground in crypts.

I stood there on the porch puzzled, confused, and reliving in a flash my life since I got to Louisiana. Since I'd moved here, this old house had unfolded one mystery after another. I found a hall closet that was an entryway to a non-existent basement, and my bedroom wall turned out to be an entryway into a hidden room. What else would I find in this house that my Aunt Pauline left me?

At that moment, I felt myself missing my old life in the big city of New York, especially the predictability of that life. Not to mention the awesome smells of the bakery around the corner from my condominium, my special spa days where I felt like I was queen for the day, the continuous hustle and bustle of the city, the wonderful shopping, and a splendid life of money, food, and drink. Ah, Sarah, you had it all, living the good life, I thought. Yep, no worries at all except for my job and how to spend my money.

It's funny how when life throws you a curveball, your thoughts become negative. Considering early this morning, I'd been thanking my lucky stars I was in Louisiana.

I did my best to stay out of everyone's way by hiding out in a dark corner of the huge empty front porch. Chills shook my body even though in reality it was probably ninety degrees in the middle of the night. Maybe it was the adrenaline of finding the body, or just the sheer shock and fright of seeing something so grotesque as that skeletal apparition. It's doubtful I'd ever forget that horrendous face staring blankly at me in the dark corner of the basement. It was like a scene from a horror movie, only I was living the horror story right now.

I raised my hand to my mouth as I tried to keep the rising nausea down.

The only thing to keep me from running from the house screaming was the darkness of the night, and the constant activity back and forth from the front door to the steps of the porch and back as I watched with this terrible feeling of being totally and utterly alone and confused by everything since I'd moved in.

Why would the condo angel direct me to a house that had so much unrest, a house that had a mystery in every corner, a house with no peace? Every day seemed to be one odd thing after another happening here. What had I gotten myself into?

Everyone I talked to considered my Aunt Pauline to be a recluse with strange and unusual habits.

Everything was so different here; the unusual heat and dampness, the culture, this terrible, sinister feeling of nature all around—it made me feel as if I had been abandoned on a lonely planet with no instruction manual on how to survive.

My life in New York was ordinary and predictable. I knew day to day what would happen. Then one day out of the blue my life transformed into an unpredictable dishevel of one disaster after another.

Sarah, you need to get a hold of yourself. That's enough negative thoughts, I tried to tell myself. It hadn't been all bad. There had been some good here.

I slowly smiled, remembering how I met Jessie on the dock at his house and how he 'took my breath away' every time he touched me or looked at me in his special way. Jessie was one of the good things.

Jessie seemed to come into my life at the right time. He filled this void in me and made my life complete. It felt great knowing he was there. He'd made the transition from New York to Louisiana bearable.

I wondered at that moment if it was possible that life is planned out in advance before we are born, or if it's all by chance? How much free-will do we really have, or do unknown forces constantly guide us to our next chapter in life?

Surely, we have help in this world. Something or someone has to be guiding us, right? After all, I was directed here by an angel.

I could have stayed in New York and ended up in low-income housing, working for minimum wage somewhere. Would I have learned the things I've learned here if I would have stayed in New York? Would God have sent me another Jessie in New York to help me?

I touched my temple, feeling a headache coming on as my mind continued to overload my senses.

Maybe it would be best if I just let life run its course the way Jessie does and stop trying to analyze it before this pain in my head burst my head in two.

At that moment, I felt someone grab my arm from the darkness of the porch. I jumped and almost screamed.

"It's okay, honey, it's just me."

"Oh Jessie," I sighed as I threw my arms around his neck.

"You're shaking. Would you like me to get you some water?"

"No, no, I'm fine. You just caught me daydreaming about this house and my unpredictable life."

"They are wrapping it all up now. The body is being sent to the coroner's office temporarily until we can make a decision about what to do next."

"Thank God. They have been here forever." I sighed. "Does anyone have any idea who that is?" I asked as I laid my head on Jessie's chest for comfort.

"Gerald doesn't want to speculate yet until they analyze everything. But…"

I raised my head to look into Jessie's eyes.

"But what?" I asked, not knowing if I really wanted to know.

"Well… we both feel it is your Aunt Pauline."

"Oh no! It couldn't be… Could it?"

"The corpse is wearing women's clothes, your Aunt Pauline's clothes."

"Did she get locked down there?" I hated to ask, but... "Was she murdered?"

"I will not lie to you, Sarah, but... it's a possibility. But it is also possible she was sick or had a heart attack and just couldn't make it back up the ladder."

I stood holding Jessie as the gurney with a black zip-up bag was rolled off the porch and into the back of an ambulance, followed by an array of people.

The shock of finding out that it may very well be my Aunt Pauline put me in such a state, that all I could see was a smeared light show of colored uniformed figures walking back and forth from my house. Dazed and in shock, the noise slowly subsided as one vehicle after another, pulled out of the driveway leaving only quiet. That is until Gerald came strolling over to stand beside Jessie.

Gerald's mouth moved, but no sound followed. I strained to hear what was being said, but to no avail.

Jessie shook me. "Sarah, Sarah... are you okay?"

Finally, the volume control slowly came back along with my mind, which had taken a hiatus to another place.

"I'm sorry, what did you say?" I heard my mouth say with a thick tongue.

"It's all right, Sarah. I'm sorry, but we feel the body you found in the cellar is your Aunt Pauline. According to the coroner, it looks like she may have had a heart attack. I'm sorry for your loss. Now you two get some rest." Gerald tipped the brim of his cap and turned to walk away.

Gerald's footsteps slowly faded into the night, leaving only quiet. Jessie and I stood there holding each other as the world seemed to stop turning. For just a moment, the swamps became quiet and the only comforting noise was Jessie's breathing. The same breathing, I had listened to each night since he'd moved in to help, the same breath that calmed my spirit and held me close at night, the same breath that kissed me good night every night.

I'm not sure I would have made it if it wasn't for Jessie.

"Thank you, God, for Jessie," I whispered.

Jessie and I lingered on the porch in the still of the night long enough so I could get the courage to go back in. After several minutes of quiet, we walked into the house in each other's arms to find such a mess that my heart sank deep in my chest.

Along with all the clothes and boxes from the closet still strewn around the living room, there were empty coffee cups and tracked mud all the way out the front door, thanks to the foot of smelly, nasty water in the basement.

Jessie cupped my face in his gentle hands and said, "I know what you're thinking, Sarah. I promise you, it will be here later to deal with. We need to get some rest. It's been a long night."

I stood there trying to fight my inner OCD demon.

"Come on, Cher; let us go warm-up that bed," Jessie said in a Cajun accent as he gently guided me towards the bedroom and away from the mess.

Jessie always knew how to lighten my mood. His Cajun accent tickled me and helped me realize he was right; it was late, close to midnight. I felt drained and numb inside as if I had been in a daze the whole afternoon and was just now coming to.

When I laid my head on Jessie's chest that night and heard his rhythmic breathing, I slowly drifted off to a wonderful dreamless sleep.

CHAPTER 3

It felt like I'd just gone to sleep when I heard soft footsteps and the smell of strong coffee and then a gentle touch on my arm, waking me.

"I don't know how you do it, Sarah."

"What?"

"How can you look so good after all we went through last night?"

It hit me like a ton of bricks and I bolted to a sitting position. There was a dead woman in the basement last night.

The memory of her face with the dark sunken holes in her head for eyes sent chills through me; the long, white, mangled hair that hung over her shoulder caused me to shudder. That horrendous sight would surely haunt me forever.

Jessie sat on the edge of the bed, still holding my coffee. "It's okay, sweetheart. It's over and done with, and I'm sure that your Aunt Pauline can rest now."

"Yeah, I know. It's just… her face."

"I know, boo, but let's not think about it. Here, drink your coffee," Jessie said, handing me a steaming cup of brew.

After my first sip, I basked in the awesomely strong, full flavor of the dark warm drink coating my throat.

I had to admit, this area had some of the best coffee I had ever had.

By my second sip, I realized I had a lot to clean up in the house after all that ruckus from last night.

"Well, boo, it looks like things can finally go back to normal," Jessie announced.

"If only that would be true. I sure hope you're right. It's been a long, difficult time since I moved in and I'm trying to be optimistic, but I guess it will be over for me when we get more info about the body—and if nothing else happens," I explained.

"Absolutely," Jessie said.

"Jessie, promise me... you will take it easy today? You don't want to end up back in the emergency room again, do you?"

"I've learned my lesson. Of course, I'll take it easy. You know me."

"Yeah, that's why I asked. The doctor said no work for at least a month. Gunshots don't heal if you don't take it easy."

We both gave each other a devious smile as Jessie stood up from the bed and bent down to place a warm kiss on my forehead.

He started walking out of the room and announced, "Don't worry about me. I have a plan."

Frustrated, I yelled, "That's what I'm afraid of."

By the time the coffee kicked in good, I had dressed and was ready to tackle that dreaded hall closet.

Jessie peeked in on me and asked, "What do you say I line up someone to fill in that basement with dirt when things cool down and before the water seeps back in again?"

I hesitated. "Well, maybe one day, but not anytime soon."

"Your wish is my command," he replied and bowed at the waist.

I walked to the hall closet and stared at it. It felt like the mystery of this house wasn't over yet, and I still wanted to investigate the basement on my own.

"Jessie, what is this yellow tape doing across the door?"

"Oh, I forgot to tell you. Gerald said the closet is off-limits for now until he can get some investigators out here too... you know... investigate."

"Damn," I whispered. "Can I at least clean the floor?"

"I think that would be all right," he said, his lip curling up on one side.

Keeping busy and cleaning kept my mind off the horrendous night we just had and my OCD demon was being fed, so everything felt calm.

There still was this nagging feeling that my life would never be at rest again until we knew for sure what had happened to Aunt Pauline. And most of all, when that piss poor excuse for a husband, Hank, was jailed in some maximum-security prison far away from here and we could finally be divorced. I wanted that man out of my life for good. The sooner the better.

What the hell was I thinking when I married him? I guess you just never really know someone. I'd had no idea he'd married me just to juice me like a grape. To get every red cent I earned. To think, he talked me into putting everything in his name while I paid for it. Was I that desperate to have a man that I would let him walk all over me like that? "Never again!" I demanded as my fist hit the wall.

Jessie yelled from the kitchen that breakfast was ready and I came back to the reality of the present.

I pulled out the old flimsy wooden chair and buttered my toast and asked, "Do you think the reason I saw Aunt Pauline by the closet so often was her trying to tell me she was in the basement?"

"Yeah, that sounds about right. All I know about ghosts is they have their own agenda. For instance, I believe the reason my parents show up at my house at sunset on the dock is not for them... It's for me."

"I think that, too, Jessie. I think they love you so much they bridge the gap of space and time just for you. After all, you said, 'where there is love, there are miracles,' right?"

"You got that right, boo." Jessie reached over and squeezed my hand.

Jessie's hand lingered a moment, and my heart exploded with love as I looked into his eyes. "Jessie, honey, I... I really love you, you know?"

"I know... I love you, too."

We were so caught up in the moment of just being with each other that we both jumped when someone knocked on the front door.

"It must be Gerald," I said.

I followed behind Jessie at a safe distance. After last night, and all the other stuff that had happened in this house, I was afraid to even venture to the front door alone. When Jessie opened the door, it surprised me to see two clean-cut men in nice dress clothes. Not your usual sight around the swamps.

"We are looking for Sarah Hamilton. Do we have the right residence?" the young dark-haired man asked.

I stepped from behind Jessie. "Yes, I'm Sarah."

"We are from the Federal Bureau of Investigation. We are here to take a look at the crime scene," the man said, showing us his credentials.

Jessie looked at me and I looked at him with our eyes widened.

"Sheriff of Avoyelles has requested our help in solving a possible murder case," the young man announced.

Murder? So they suspect murder. As much as I hated the thought of my Aunt Pauline murdered I knew in my heart it was true. Why else would a body be sitting in a chair in the dark corner of the basement?

"May we come in?"

"Yes, sure, I'm sorry, please come in," Jessie said, opening the door wider and moving back to allow them entry.

Jessie pointed to the hall closet where the yellow tape had barred my attempt to investigate the cellar for my own curiosity.

As the young man with darker hair walked towards the closet, the man with the salt and pepper hair standing behind him asked, "May I ask you some questions?"

"Yes, of course." I looked around and saw there was no place to sit comfortably in the living room since everything was still in disarray.

"Please, follow us to the kitchen."

Jessie and I walked past the closet to the kitchen as I watched the young man remove the yellow tape and lift the closet floor lid to the basement.

Jessie immediately started cleaning off the table from our late breakfast and offered the man some coffee.

"No, thanks. I need to get to the business at hand. My name is Special Agent Ray Logan."

We watched as Ray took out a small notebook from his pocket and began to write.

"I'm sorry; sir, but I don't understand what the FBI has to do with this case. It's a local matter, not Federal."

"What you may not know about your Aunt is that she was a trusted undercover FBI employee for many years and then a trustworthy informant for many years after that."

My mouth dropped. "Are you sure you're talking about Pauline Bordelon?"

"Yes indeed, only she worked under another name for her protection."

I sat back in my chair, dumbfounded. The room got so quiet you could have heard an ant walk across the floor.

"May I ask what her alias was?"

"Her name was Elizabeth Henry." My mind jolted with a spark of remembrance.

That name sounded familiar. Where did I hear that name from? Then it hit me.

"Did she by any chance work some in New York?"

"Yes. Lizzie, I mean Elizabeth, worked in many places, and New York was one of her favorites. She loved New York because it gave her the opportunity to look you up."

My mouth fell open and my heart raced as my memory kicked into overdrive. "Oh my, I met her. I remember... she had some dealings with my advertising firm. She took me to lunch once after closing on an advertising deal. I can't remember which company she worked for off the top of my head, but I liked her from day one. We really hit it off. How do you know all this?" I asked Ray, still in shock.

With a crooked smile and a raised eyebrow, Ray replied, "Mrs. Hamilton, there is not too much we don't know. Your Aunt and I worked closely together for years, and we were good friends. I remember her talking about you. She was so excited to know she had a niece. That's how you ended up with this house. Once she retired, she took back her original name. She bought this house from the old man who migrated here from France back in the late eighteen to the early nineteen-hundreds."

A knot formed in my throat. I was speechless and couldn't believe I had met my Aunt and didn't even know it. And to realize this house was over a hundred years old. It also made me wonder if the hidden passageway had been built back then or added by my Aunt, given what I had just learned about her profession.

So, my eccentric elderly Aunt was probably just a smart old coot that wanted the town's people to think she'd slid off her cracker, but apparently in reality she was a brilliant undercover agent. The corner of my mouth flipped up as I tried to subdue laughter.

Ray continued, "It's really a long story, but the old man was under the witness protection act and your Aunt's first case was to keep him safe. I can't give you the specific details seeing as how that's confidential still, but they became good friends and the man sold your Aunt this house before he went into the nursing home."

"Do you remember the old man's name?" Jessie asked.

"Yes, his last name was St. Pierre. It has been many years. If I can recall correctly, your Aunt found this basement when she first bought the place. She didn't occupy the house for many years, but said there was something about the place that called to her and she had to have it. So, to make a long story short, we are here to cover all our bases and make sure there are no more loose ends. The basement is our primary concern today. We have techniques and equipment used to solve murders that your local police department doesn't have access to."

Jessie spoke up. "I worked for Miss Pauline for years and never knew she had a basement. I took for granted the bricks under the house were from an old fireplace that they left up for support. I know back in the day fireplaces were centrally located for heating purposes, so I didn't pay any mind to it. As far as I knew she renovated this place and put bricks for beam support. I never questioned her. I know that the fireplace in the living room is newer than the house."

"How do you know?" Ray asked.

"The bricks are newer, plus I passed by here on the way to school my whole life, and even though there never seemed to be anyone living here for many years, there was always someone keeping up the yard and house until I got back from college. Then I became the handyman."

I sat there wondering if the fireplace could be yet another mystery.

"Would you know, Ray, why Aunt Pauline didn't tell me who she was?" I asked.

"She was undercover and it would have been dangerous to you and to any case she was handling. She always had the intention of looking you up again one day, but decided against it. Lizzie, I mean Pauline—always felt that something just wasn't right. As long as I knew her, she said she felt like she was being watched. Of course, it's always better to be safe than sorry in this business. You can never be too careful."

"Do you feel Sarah is in danger living here?" Jessie asked, concern written all over his face.

Ray hesitated. "We should know soon if you have anything to worry about. Now, I have some questions, Sarah. Have you experienced any strange activities in the house beside the break-ins from your husband and his accomplice?"

There was no way I was going to tell the FBI about the ghost of Aunt Pauline. "So you know about Hank?" I asked.

"As I said, there is not too much we don't know."

"Well, to answer your question, no, just Hank wanting this house for the supposed treasure it holds."

"Yes, well…. we've heard of the rumor of money or treasure here."

"Is it possible there is any truth to this rumor?" I bit my lower lip in anticipation of his answer.

"Don't you worry. At present, we feel there is nothing to substantiate that claim," Ray said as he stood up.

I don't know why, but I felt there was something he wasn't telling me.

The investigation of the basement went on for hours.

"What in the world is taking them so long?" I whispered to Jessie.

"They're just being thorough, I guess. They'll be out of here in no time," he said with confidence.

CHAPTER 4

It was afternoon before the two FBI agents finally drug themselves out of the basement, wet and dirty from head to foot.

I struggled to contain my laughter. Two well-dressed FBI agents went in and two dirty men came out. "They sure were prepared for the job," I announced and hit Jessie in the ribs with my elbow while snickering.

We both turned away from the men to smile and giggle with one another.

I heard someone clear their throat behind us, and that put a stop to our playtime. "Sorry for the mess, but we have all we need. If we need anything further, we will let you know."

Ray picked up two duffel bags, full of evidence I guessed, and walked out the door.

When I closed the door behind the agents, I turned and broke out into uncontrollable laughter that had Jessie joining me in the humor of it all.

"They sure got a lot of evidence. Head to toe evidence." At that point, tears were streaming down my cheeks. "Did you see those slacks they had on? They had mud and water up to their knees. They will have to throw them away after today's investigation." I giggled and made air quotes as I drawled out the word investigation.

Jessie came to me and pulled me close as his laughter eased into a smile. After a last snort, my laughter subsided, and I looked deep into Jessie's eyes with a desire for his lips on mine.

As his sweet warm breath swept across my forehead, I raised my face to meet his kiss.

His kiss was tender and alluring. It was like we could close the chapter on the past couple of days and we were free to enjoy each other without further commotion; all the dark baggage of death was gone.

He slowly pulled me closer with each minute of his kiss. My legs grew weak, and I yearned to be one with him.

"Sarah," he whispered in my ear. "Sarah," he whispered again as he clutched the mounds of my butt cheeks, pulling me to him in a smoldering desire that was unfolding between us.

"Sarah, I want you so bad it hurts." Jessie moaned as his warm hands released their grip and slid up my back under my shirt, caressing my skin.

His warm hands sent chills through me as my breathing became labored.

"Jessie, make love to me." I moaned with a deep heat of desire that needed to be fulfilled.

Jessie's hands slowly slid out from under my shirt and cupped my face with a tender kiss.

"There is nothing I want more than to throw caution to the wind and have you right here, right now, but… I just can't right now. Like I've said before, technically, you're still married. You understand, don't you?"

With a sigh of regret, I said, "Yes, I know."

I released my hold on him as my heart deflated like a balloon, disappointed and yet happy to know he wanted me as much as I wanted him.

He grabbed my arm as I walked away. "Please don't be mad."

"How can I be mad? I love you. I'm willing to wait as long as it takes."

With a wink and a smile, he offered to help me clean up the mess the two FBI agents left, plus all the clutter that had taken up residence in the living room over the past several days.

I watched Jessie grab the broom and mop. "Okay, I'll clean the floors while you sift through your Aunt's stuff."

I was glad he'd offered to clean the floor from all the mud from the two well-organized FBI agents, Tweedledee and Tweedledum came to investigate.

Sitting on the floor, making sure all paperwork was put back in the box, I watched Jessie. His shaggy dark brown hair hung in his eyes as he lifted the dustpan from the floor. The muscles on his arms and chest protruded through his thin, tight, tee-shirt, and I couldn't help but stare in awe of his stature. He towered over my five foot four frame with a body that was rock hard as though he was some kind of weight lifter or something.

After several hours of cleaning and putting all the clothes and boxes back in the closet, Jessie asked if I was ready for a trip to his house, which had become a daily thing lately.

I looked at my watch and realized the sun would go down soon and we didn't like to miss the exceptional sunset and the accompanying mystical show.

"Are you sure you feel strong enough to go today?"

With a quick look at the wall clock, he announced, "Let's go." He grabbed my hand as we walked out the back door and down to the boat dock.

We always enjoyed the boat ride and the ghostly appearance of his parents on the dock at sunset since that first day he'd shown me.

I never tired of observing the beauty of the swamps at dusk. Every time was unique. No two sunsets were alike. It was as though God painted the landscape fresh and new every day.

Jessie held me as we sat side-by-side on the steps of his house for the best panoramic view possible.

"Do you think Aunt Pauline's ghost will go away now?" I asked.

"Yeah, I'm pretty sure she was there to get closure, and now that we have found her body I believe she can move on."

Just like clockwork, his parents came and watched the sunset with us. The apparition of Jessie's parents melted into the darkness, and he took my hand as we walked down to the end of the dock.

"Sarah, these last several months with you have been the best times of my life. I don't want it to ever end."

"Me too, Jessie." I cleared my throat. "I want to thank you."

"For what?" he asked as he put his arm around me.

"You know… for giving up your life here at your house and moving in with me until all this stuff has settled."

"Sarah, you are my life now. What I do for you, I also do for me. You make me happy."

With that statement, he picked me up and twirled me round and round.

"Jessie, put me down before we both fall into the bayou," I screamed through laughter.

My heart nearly exploded with joy. All these years trying to fill this void in my life with expensive merchandise and trying to please Hank had just been a waste of time. But now I felt like there was nothing I could ever want more than Jessie. He would always be my knight and shining armor. Life with him would satisfy me like no other I could imagine.

As we settled down that night in my cozy bed all I could feel was love and how it was the one piece of the puzzle of my life that I'd never had.

I snuggled closer to Jessie and nuzzled up to his neck and could already hear his rhythmic breathing, which calmed my soul each night. He was already asleep.

It didn't take long to join him in that wonderful slumber.

At some time in the night, I turned over away from Jessie and was awakened by a cold, damp spot on the bed.

"What the hell..." I whispered groggily, trying to push myself up and away from the wet spot.

It was dark and warm in the room with just a small breeze from a fan hitting my skin. As my eyes adjusted all I could see was something dark on the white sheets of my bed.

I reached over and grabbed a small flashlight from my bedside table, and careful not to wake Jessie, I turned it on to see what was on the bed.

I gasped as I saw blood. Frantically, I searched to see if Jessie's gunshot wound had bled but noticed there was no blood around him.

Jessie moved and turned over on his side and I sat still, hoping I hadn't disturbed him.

Once I was sure he wasn't waking up, I searched the bed to see where the blood was coming from.

I got out of the bed and noticed that there was a pool of blood on the floor by my feet.

Trying not to hyperventilate into a panic attack, I forcefully calmed my breathing to a strong and steady flow. I told myself I would not go into a total freak out in the middle of the night.

Slowly, I straddled the blood and followed it since it seemed to be headed around the bed to the opposite wall where the secret panel was.

As I examined the secret panel, I saw blood oozing from beneath the floorboard to the entrance.

"What are you doing?" I heard from behind me.

I jumped, and the flashlight went flying from my hands.

"What's the matter?" I heard as I turned slowly, hoping the voice was Jessie and not someone else.

Jessie leaned over and turned on the lamp on the night table on his side of the bed, illuminating the room.

"I... I..." was all that would come from my mouth as I struggled to find something to say when I noticed that the blood had disappeared when Jessie turned on the light.

I must have been dreaming. Where did all the blood go?

I felt Jessie's arms slowly tighten around me as he walked me back to my side of the bed.

He took a shortcut straddling over me into bed, then pulling the sheet back up tucking me back in. Nice and cozy. He whispered groggily, "Go back to sleep, boo."

What the hell just happened? If there was no blood, then where was I going?

Jessie kissed my forehead, snuggling close with his arm over my body. I couldn't help but feel safe and secure once again. I grinned, wondering if he was showing how much he cared by holding me so close or was he holding me down so I didn't get up to go investigating in the middle of the night again.

CHAPTER 5

When morning came and I was sitting up drinking my coffee in bed with Jessie, which was a normal routine now. I wondered if he would mention last night.

I didn't have to wonder long.

"What were you doing last night?" Jessie asked, concern evident in his tone.

"I think… I think I heard a mouse in the house last night. I thought it came from your side of the room."

I couldn't believe I'd just lied to the man I loved, but what else could I say? Could I tell him I was hallucinating about blood coming from the secret panel? Or that I was possibly sleepwalking around the room, which is something I've never done before?

All I knew is that in the pit of my stomach I felt the mystery of the house was not solved just yet.

"I can check that out this morning and run to the store and get some traps. Don't worry, if we have mice, they won't be here long."

"That would be great."

I sipped my coffee as I went over in my head how once he left for the store I would examine the floor closely and make sure there was nothing I was missing.

I watched as Jessie finished up his coffee and took my empty cup and left the room for the kitchen sink.

I pulled back the bedspread and saw nothing out of the ordinary. Glancing onto the floor, all I saw were my slippers, which I never wore anyway. The floor looked clean and there wasn't even the slightest sign of blood anywhere.

Jessie walked in, kissed me lightly, and informed me he would be back shortly.

Once I was sure he'd left, I walked over to the secret panel and opened it. The side-wall opened while I grabbed the flashlight and slipped on some shoes. It still amazed me that there was no way of telling there was a secret passageway behind the wall. Whoever built it must have been a genius to hide something so masterfully in plain sight.

Even though I'd been in the secret passage several times before, I was never alone. The dirt and thoughts of creepy-crawly always gave me the willies. I stood still momentarily as the word 'alone' kept repeating in my mind, trying to keep me from my task.

It was dark and musty as I took a deep breath and ventured in.

Being careful not to touch the sides of the narrow hallway leading to the ladder, something caught my eye. It was a slight reflection ahead of me between the slats of the ladder. What is that, I wonder? I'd never noticed it before. I kept moving the flashlight up and down the wall behind the ladder to focus my sight on the shiny object.

There, there it was. It looked like a tiny piece of rusty metal about the size of a small fingernail file.

I hesitantly reached out to grab the metal and my hand hit a spider web which made me jump back as chills ran all the way down my body.

I regained my composure, used the flashlight to remove any other webs and felt for the piece of metal again.

I pulled and pushed, trying to get it to move. Then I decided to slide it to the left, and it gave way to a tiny hole. Gingerly leaning forward, trying not to get my face too close to the dusty ladder slats, I noticed some light. Finally, I gave in and put my face between the slats of the ladder to get a closer look… and there it was. It was an excellent view of the hallway by the closet. Wow, a hidden peephole.

It amazed me how a house this old could have so many unusual anomalies.

Curiosity got the best of me and I looked for other out the ordinary things on the wall; not like the hidden room wasn't out of the ordinary already.

I found nothing, so climbed the stairs to the hidden room above. After shaking my body like a dog after a bath and using the flashlight to make sure I didn't get any dirt or spider webs on me, I began a search of the walls.

I couldn't believe it. Right by the ladder was another rusty piece of metal. When I slid it open, I got another excellent view of the hallway upstairs. Even though I had been in the house several months I never really examined the upstairs area for anything unusual. I only gave the place a cursory look around when I first moved in, but nothing seemed out-of-place upstairs in the three bedrooms, so why bother going over every inch. Everything I needed was downstairs, so I hadn't felt the need to venture elsewhere.

I couldn't believe my luck finding the peepholes. Unless you knew to look for them, I could have lived here my whole life and never suspected. How strange that I would come across them now.

"Hmm, I wonder if there is anything else I might find up here," I whispered to myself as I swept the flashlight across the old boards nailed up around the wall to make this small hideout of a room.

I saw no more metal of any kind, so I stood back from the wall trying to get a better view. My eye caught sight of a small square-shaped piece of wood that didn't fit the pattern of the other long boards along the wall. How unusual, I thought, scratching my head. If it would have been a snake, it would have bitten me. I was tickled pink to not only find something else unusual, but I had heard Jessie use that saying before, and there I was saying it, too. Was this just a patch-up job or is there something behind it?

Do I really want to know what this means? I'm supposed to be looking for blood. Not another secret in this house?

Slowly and cautiously, I pressed my hand on the small, out-of-place panel. It gave way under the pressure and I heard a click. Removing my hand, the panel opened up. Inside was a simple latch. I lifted the latch, and the wall moved open into the empty hallway upstairs.

"What the hell?" My mouth fell open. "Aunt Pauline, what in the world were you up to in this house?"

I couldn't help but wonder why a retired FBI agent would have a house with so many extraordinary secrets. Had she really retired? Did she need to hide from someone? Is that why there were secret rooms in this house? Was there really hidden treasure here? Who was this strange woman—and who'd killed her?

"I wonder if I'll ever get the answers," I mumbled as I closed the hidden wall and latched it back.

I was standing there in deep thought when I heard a car pull up outside. That must be Jessie, I thought.

As fast as I could I made my way back to the bedroom and closed the secret wall just as Jessie walked in the room.

"Hey, you're not dressed yet. What are you up to?" Jessie asked as he moved closer to me.

Do I tell him about the secrets I just found? How do I explain going into the secret room without him?

I left well enough alone and decided not to mention my adventure. "I'm just being lazy and was looking for a mouse hole," I lied again.

What was wrong with me? I hated lying like this. But, I couldn't shake this feeling of impending doom pressing on my heart and I just didn't want to confide in Jessie, at least not right now. He needed to get well from his gunshot wound. Plus, we'd had so much happen in this house in such a short period of time. I just didn't want to burden him with my bloody dream and my new findings in the secret passageway. He needed rest, and that's all there was to it.

As I dressed, Jessie put some mousetraps out, and then we had a slow, leisurely day. I was thankful for the downtime after all the recent commotion. I was definitely ready for a day full of nothing. At least I had hoped for that.

It was around three in the afternoon when someone came knocking on our door.

To no surprise to me, it was the local sheriff in town, Gerald.

"Come in, Gerald, and have a seat. I'll get you a cup of Joe." I smiled and motioned him to sit in the living room. "I'll get Jessie. He is sitting on the back porch."

"Oh, that's okay. I'll greet him there," Gerald said as he walked with me to the kitchen. I grabbed a cup from the cupboard as Gerald made his way to the back porch.

I could hear them speaking in an unusual low tone of their ancestral language, Cajun French, as I poured some strong brew. Gerald had become a member of the family since all the mysteries of the house started unraveling, so I knew exactly how he liked his coffee. It calmed my spirit to hear the two of them speaking on the porch. But I found it unusual that they seemed to speak more French than usual.

When I walked onto the porch with Gerald's hot mug, they reverted back to English, I presumed on my account.

It was a nice day, not as sticky since the rain passed. The sun was bright and there were only some residual clouds in the sky. There was a slight ripple on the water from the breeze and there was just a beautiful hint of fall in the air.

Jessie said summer lasted for at least seven to eight months, then you had fall for two weeks till winter, which lasted just a couple of months. He told me that there have been many Christmas parties with flip-flops and tee-shirts, but not to count on that because there have been cold fronts to come in as early as the middle of October and end as late as March. He laughed and said summer was a staring match, and spring, fall, and winter were only a blink. It took me a while to understand his humor about the seasons, but then I understood the staring match with summer was because it lasted so long. Duh.

I sat next to Jessie on the porch swing as we both watched Gerald sip his hot coffee on an old chair that looked like it couldn't hold a five-pound bag of sugar.

Jessie broke the silence. "What brings you out today?"

Gerald set the coffee cup on the floor and rubbed his face.

I held my breath. I knew that was a sign of stalling while he figured out how to tell us whatever it was.

"I, I caught Hank last night just outside your property."

I stood up abruptly. "You can't be serious? You have got to be kidding me... right?"

"I wouldn't joke about something like that, Sarah."

"I thought maybe he found a way back to New York," I said, twisting my hands nervously.

"Afraid not, Sarah. The judge ordered him to stay in town until his court date or stay in jail," Gerald whispered, his head held low, not wanting to look me in the eyes.

"So, did you arrest him for trespassing?" I demanded.

Gerald raised his head, disappointment etched on his face. "I had nothing to hold him on. Technically, he wasn't on your property."

Jessie put his hand on my arm. "It will be okay, I'm still here. He won't get past me."

"Yeah, well, he got past you last time with a gun," I shouted, my anger at the situation exploding.

Jessie's face dropped. He knew it was true. He was as helpless at gunpoint as I was.

"Hank is in a lot of trouble and he would be stupid to call attention to himself again," Gerald explained.

"Exactly," Jessie agreed. "What about that so-called attorney, Brian? Is he still in cahoots with Hank?" Jessie asked.

"As far as I know Brian has been staying low and out the way. Again, he better watch his P's and Q's, because I'm watching him," Gerald demanded.

"What a crooked lawyer," I muttered under my breath.

Gerald and Jessie both nodded.

"Any word on the body we found in the basement?" Jessie inquired.

"No, not yet. The FBI took the body back with them for a more thorough check with DNA, dental, and whatever else they use. They said a small town like Marksville just doesn't have the equipment that they do. In fact, it was kind of funny how they just swooped in here uninvited and took over the investigation. I figured it was because Pauline was a part of their team."

"Yeah, I gathered that, too. Only… they said you invited them here," I said, boring holes into Gerald's eyes for answers.

"Really? Since a murder has to go through certain channels, I figured they saw the address and pounced on it because of your Aunt. But no, I did not technically invite them. They seem to have eyes everywhere. I wouldn't be surprised if they were bugging our conversation now."

"What? You can't be serious!" I yelled.

With a slight grin and wink at Jessie, Gerald said, "So, Jessie tells me you took my advice and used the lawyer I recommended to start your divorce proceedings."

"That's not funny, Gerald," I said through gritted teeth. "But, uh, yes I did. He was very confident since we have been separated longer than six months with no kids and with some persuasion, I can keep my house and be done with him in a matter of months."

"He even said that its possible Hank might consider relinquishing his rights to Pauline's property in exchange for a more lenient sentence," Jessie announced.

"If only it could be that easy," I said, knowing Hank would not give up on a house he believed to hold a fortune in money and jewels.

"Anything is possible, Sarah. We can always negotiate the terms of his jail time if he signs the divorce papers," Gerald said with a wink. "You see... I know people, too." Gerald flashed an evil grin that made me laugh.

Jessie smiled. "Sounds like we have a plan."

"Well, I've got work to do. Thanks for the coffee, Sarah." Gerald tipped the brim of his cap and walked down the stairs and around the house to the front where his patrol car was parked.

I looked at Jessie. "If only it would go that easy."

"Don't count your alligators before they hatch, Sarah. You just never know the persuasion of Gerald and his contacts."

CHAPTER 6

It was always wonderful sleeping with the man I loved. The comfort and security I felt gave me a deep and abiding feeling of love beyond anything Hank ever had. Hank was there, but not in the same capacity as Jessie. Hank was a warm body, sure, but the feelings were nowhere near the same.

After our ritual of morning coffee, Jessie suggested we go to the courthouse and look up the information on the original owner of the house.

Excited to see what we might find, I agreed and went to take a quick look in the mirror before we left, eyeing myself from every angle. Making sure my long brown, wavy hair was in place and my green eyes popped with the new eye shadow I was trying out. Just because I was in the country didn't mean I had to look like a bum, I told myself as I looked over my shoulder at my tight-fitting blue jeans and the curves of my body. I was positive the three-inch heels I was wearing would add considerable height to my five-foot, four inches. I was looking good for an outing on the town. I grabbed my purse and ran to the porch to find Jessie waiting patiently for me.

"You know we are only going to the courthouse records department, right?" Jessie asked, his eyebrows cocked quizzically.

"Of course, I know that. Don't you like the way I'm dressed?"

Jessie's eyes widened, and he ran his fingers through his hair, clearing his throat at the same time. "You look wonderful," he said, turning from me and readjusting the front of his pants.

I smiled. I still got it, I thought. I hadn't had that effect on a man in a while. I should never let myself become complacent just because I lived in the swamps.

The day was gorgeous. There was a slight breeze from the north blowing through the leaves, and for once there didn't seem to be much humidity. I was thankful that, perhaps, my hair wouldn't be frizzy.

We made it to the courthouse square in the center of town. There didn't seem to be a parking spot within a two-block radius.

"I guess they're having court today," Jessie uttered.

The courthouse stood in the center of town surrounded by restaurants, small clothing stores, a barbershop, a dog groomer, a bank, and several other establishments. It was your typical small town, along with all its charm.

I grinned because it made me feel like I'd stepped back in time to witness a place you would find in an old black and white movie. The people seemed to be your everyday Joe; from the courthouse, lawyers dressed in their finest markdown suits all the way to the farmers dressed in their best blue jeans and overalls. It still amazed me how dressed down the people in the south were compared to New Yorkers.

I shrugged my shoulders and guessed it was because they considered this area to be swamps, country, or whatever.

Once we made it inside, that's where things changed. I was confused because the old black and white town in the fifties movie outside, transformed into a prime time reality show of the twentieth century with a total lockdown of security inside. It almost made me feel like I'd walked into another world. A world I wasn't familiar with.

Where had the old-time, small-town charm gone to? When had I transported to the future of lockdown?

"Excuse me, ma'am, you're holding up the line," a prison guard barked out at me.

Jessie pulled me in further as the guard motioned me to walk through the metal detector.

After the humiliation of an "almost," strip search we got past the door into the hallway and Jessie leaned and whispered in my ear, "I remember back in the day when you could walk into any door of this building freely and get your business done. But now, it's like Fort Knox with red tape to get things taken care of. The many always seem to suffer because of the few."

I nodded in agreement. I never gave it much thought, but laws and things changed because someone couldn't or wouldn't obey the rules.

As we made our way to the records section, I felt like everyone was watching us as we passed each counter. Even worse was once we were deep among the shelves, I had the distinct feeling that someone was boring holes in my back.

I turned to find an overweight man staring at me. What is he looking at? Oh, maybe it's because I'm overdressed for this part of the world.

I looked again, and he was still staring at me. I pressed in closer to Jessie for protection. This man's eyes didn't look like someone just looking at a pretty lady, but more like someone contemplating a crime. I wanted to run right back out the way we came.

As I looked around for an escape route, I realized how dingy everything was from the ceiling to the floors. It didn't look like they had renovated since around the forties.

"How old is this place?" I whispered, hoping not to draw attention.

"If I remember correctly, they built it back in 1927."

"Yeah, I can tell," I replied.

Jessie glanced at me briefly, then looked around. He seemed unaffected by the dingy place. He was more focused on finding information about our mission than anything else.

I nosed around while Jessie got directions from a lady behind the counter.

"Come this way," Jessie said as I followed him to another area where we found some enormous books with land surveys.

After searching page after page, Jessie said, "Look here."

I followed his gaze to what seemed to be a drawing with lines that made no sense to me.

The terrible, spine-tingling feeling of being watched made me look around the room to find that same man watching me again.

Jessie continued to analyze and read, oblivious to the stranger ogling us.

He pointed out that the land was so close to Indian land that he wondered if it may have once belonged to the Indians where the casino was built.

Not paying attention to what Jessie was saying, I walked behind him to a row of shelves lined with books reaching to the ceiling as I kept my eye on the stranger.

Jessie was so engrossed in the books, turning the pages; he didn't realize I had walked away.

I watched as the man casually made his way to the opposite end of the row of books, shadowing me.

Fear gripped me even though I was in a room full of people. What did this weirdo want? Why was he following me? I wondered.

I immediately went back to Jessie and insisted we leave.

"What's wrong, Sarah?" he asked with concern.

"I… I'm feeling faint, let's go," I begged.

We made our way out the door without a search and into the sunshine, away from the dark dusty shelves and the stranger. I finally felt like I could take a breath. I inhaled deeply, clearing my lungs and my mind from the weird stalker. It felt like I had been holding my breath the whole time.

After we settled in the car, I buckled up and turned to lock the passenger side door. I looked at Jessie while he put the key in the ignition, then stopped and turned towards me.

"Now, what was that all about?" Jessie insisted.

My smile faded. "I was feeling claustrophobic in there and needed to get out… I couldn't breathe. Plus… I think… someone was watching me."

"Was it Hank?" Jessie asked.

"No, it was a stranger… a fat slob of a stranger."

"Are you sure he was watching you and not us or something else? There were a lot of people in there."

"I walked behind the shelf of books and he followed me. I'm pretty damn sure he was watching me," I insisted.

"Okay, cool down," Jessie said with a slight tilt from the corner of his mouth.

"What are you smiling about?" I yelled.

"Well… you have to admit you are a little over-dressed for a courthouse visit. You have no idea how beautiful you are, do you? I'm sure he was just getting him some eye candy."

"Don't you ever take anything seriously? After everything we have gone through in that house, you think he just wanted to gawk at me? You can't be serious." I was so mad I knew my face was turning red.

"Okay, okay, do you want me to go back in there and confront the man?"

"Don't be stupid. What if he has a gun?" I asked.

Jessie laughed and laughed. "Did you forget, we went through a metal detector and we were practically stripped searched? There is no way anyone got into that place with a gun, knife, or even a fingernail file."

"Well, okay. I guess I'm a little paranoid. But do you blame me?" I slowly raised my head at an angle, questioning him with my eyes.

"I won't let anything happen to you, boo. I promise," Jessie whispered in my ear as he leaned in for a kiss on the cheek.

Something kept eating at me. I wasn't sure if it was the stranger or if it was just my paranoia taking hold of me like the tight seat belt across my body. As we drove back to the house, my mind wouldn't stop telling me I was missing something important, like looking at a puzzle piece that is right in front of my face, only I couldn't see it and didn't know where it fit.

I was thankful that the rest of the afternoon and evening was uneventful.

That night when we snuggled up in each other's arms, we talked about the house and the previous owner. Jessie insisted that the Indians lost the land that my house was on. He said he didn't have time to prove it, but his parents told him long ago that not only my land but across the bayou and even the land his parents' house was on was Indian land. But as time went on, the Indian land shrank and shrank.

As our casual conversation went from long paragraphs to short sentences, my eyes started to close on me in mid-stream of our talk. Jessie was down to just mumbling and acknowledging my comments with an uh-huh until his rhythmic breathing started. At that time, I knew it didn't matter if my conversation was only half sentences or not. That was my cue to just drift off.

Then the dream started. The music was loud, and I watched Jessie walk away to get us some drinks. It was smoky and dark with black silhouettes all around until I noticed a man staring at me. It was dark and I couldn't make out his features.

I wondered if it was my imagination that he was looking at me. Maybe he was looking at something else.

I felt panicky being in a strange bar with people I didn't know. Slowly the man walked towards my table. I whispered in my head, please go away. Don't stop here. Just pass my table.

Unable to control the dread, I shifted uncomfortably in my seat with my head down. Where was Jessie? Why wasn't he here with me? Why did he leave me alone?

I felt as if I was moving in slow motion as I gradually raised my head to look for Jessie, while out of the corner of my eye I could see the man steadily approaching inch by inch.

My body shivered like I was outside in thirty-degree weather without a coat, and yet, I could feel sweat starting to bead up all over my body as though I was having a hot flash.

My hands gripped the chair I was seated on as the man slowly slid behind me. Part of me was so relieved that he hadn't stopped that I let out a sigh. It was so crowded that the man's enormous belly grazed my back, leaving me with a sick feeling of vomit in the back of my throat.

I awoke in a scream from the pits of hell.

Jessie sat up with a start beside me. "What's wrong? Did you have a bad dream?"

"Jessie, I know who that man was."

"What man, are you talking about?" He asked sleepily.

"The man at the courthouse, the stranger, the man who was staring at me and following me around," I said, my voice rising in volume with each word.

"Okay… okay, I remember," Jessie said, running his hands through his hair.

"Don't you remember when you took me out several weeks ago? We ate, then went to listen to music at the bar. Remember how that man came to ask me to dance and how when I turned him down, he walked behind me, dragging his fat belly across my back? That was the man from the courthouse. I knew there was something familiar about him. No wonder he followed me behind the shelves. He remembered me from that night," I said, as a chill running down my body.

"It's okay, I'm here. I told you I would let nothing happen to you and I am a man of my word. I promise I will do everything in my power to keep you safe."

"Okay, I know I'm overreacting, but he scares me."

"You will probably never see that man again. It was just by chance we ran into him today," Jessie tried consoling me.

"Oh yeah, by chance, is that what you think? Was it by chance that I lost everything in New York and inherited this house of mystery? Was it chance that Hank intercepted my mail and was breaking into this house for hidden treasure? Was it chance that we found that secret room or that we found Aunt Pauline in the cellar?" I screamed louder than I wanted to. "I seriously believe that there is no such thing as chance. Somewhere, somehow, my life has been sabotaged. I don't feel my life will ever be the same again."

Jessie pulled me close and lay back down with me. "Cher tete fae. Everything will be okay. I promise."

CHAPTER 7

I waited until I heard Jessie's breathing change, and I slipped out of bed. There was no way I could go back to sleep with the picture of that grotesque man still swimming around in my mind.

My fear was getting the best of me, and I just couldn't let Jessie get involved in my insecurities.

It was early, but not so early that I couldn't start a pot of coffee. I looked out the kitchen window while I filled the pot with water. The dawn was just minutes from transforming darkness into light. I watched as the wind moved the moss in the trees with just enough light to cast an eerie glow. My body shook as if someone had walked on my grave.

With a strong cup of Java in hand, I curled up on the old couch with a light, soft blanket to keep me warm in the fall's chill air.

I blew on my coffee and took a sip of the warm, dark roast and wondered about what Jessie said. He said he would keep me safe, and that everything would be okay. He promised.

I almost lost him when Hank shot him. How could I live here or go on if something happened to him? I could feel a tear trickling down one side of my face.

Leaning over to grab a Kleenex from the coffee table, out of the corner of my eye I saw something protruding from the corner of the back portion of Old Blue, my favorite recliner.

It looked like a worn photo album. I gasped as I realized it was Aunt Pauline's photo album.

I must have missed it when I cleaned up the living room after the FBI left.

Skimming the pages, I came to the photo of Aunt Pauline in her gaudy blue dress with her white hair cascading down one side of her body.

I couldn't get over how much like me she looked, which reminded me how much like my mom she looked, too. There was never any denying that I was my mom's daughter. How funny that I didn't remember how much we all looked alike. How strange. Guess she really was my Aunt.

As I scanned through one picture after another, it was great to watch her life progress from picture to picture. There was even a picture of Aunt Pauline and that FBI guy who talked to Jessie and me.

"Hmm, what was his name?" I wondered aloud as I pushed my hair behind my ears.

Oh yeah, Ray Logan, that was it.

As I went from page to page, gazing, and taking in everything I could about Aunt Pauline, I came across a familiar picture. It was a young Aunt Pauline clad in dress pants and shirt, standing by the corner of the front porch of this old house. I squinted and struggled to see who the blurry figure was sitting on the porch.

The shock hit me like a ton of bricks. It must have been the original owner. An old man in a wheelchair with gloomy black eyes stared out at me.

I got up and rummaged through a drawer under the bookshelf and found a magnifying glass. Excited about my discovery, I scrutinized the photo thoroughly.

I sat in a state of unbelief as I gazed out into space with my heart racing. The shock of what I was seeing made my hands tremble and my skin crawl.

It felt like someone had just hit me over the head with a two by four. With my mind racing in unbelief, I looked one more time. There was no doubt about it.

The figure on the front porch was a ghost.

I looked up from the picture to see a man standing in the archway, and I screamed.

It took me a minute or two to realize Jessie had come and sat beside me and was trying to calm me down.

"It's only me. It's okay," Jessie pleaded with me in a calm, tranquil voice.

"I, I thought you were someone else," I said, breathing heavily.

"Who did you think I was this early in the morning?"

"Well, I can't explain, so let me show you."

I handed Jessie the photo and asked, "What do you see?"

Jessie passed his hand over his face and stared at the photo. "Well, it looks like you in front of the house. But I know it couldn't be you, so maybe," he scratched his head, "I guess, it's your aunt."

"No... well, yes. Not the lady... look on the porch. Do you see something here?" I pointed.

"It looks kind of blurry."

"Here, try this," I said, handing him the magnifying glass.

"Oh, it's an elderly man in a wheelchair." Jessie was raising the photo up and down, trying to get a closer view. "He looks like he is just sitting there."

"And?" I asked eagerly for him to see what I saw.

His hands fell to his knees as he looked at me with shock. "It... it looks like a ghost."

I yelled, "Ha, ha. Ding, ding, ding! You win the grand prize. Yes." I breathed out a long, hard sigh.

"Who the hell is that?" Jessie asked as he examined my face for answers.

"Are you kidding me? I thought you would know who it was."

"No, I have no idea. I wonder if your aunt knew she was photo-bombed by an apparition."

I giggled with a snort.

Jessie's eyebrow rose, and a twinkle appeared in his eyes.

"Are there any other photos like this?"

"Not that I saw. How about you give it a look-see and I'll go pour you some coffee?"

Jessie slapped my butt as I walked past him. "Thanks, boo."

We were heavily into examining pictures for the next hour when we heard someone pull up in the driveway. Peeking through the curtains, I saw Gerald.

Opening the door and stepping back, Gerald walked in. "Comment ca va?" he said in his thick Cajun accent. Gerald laughed as he saw the blank look on my face. "How are you doing? You're up mighty early this fine morning."

"We are looking at some of Aunt Pauline's pictures and we found something very unusual," I said, closing the door behind him.

"Really?" Gerald drawled out.

"Have a seat, my friend," Jessie said, pointing at Old Blue.

"Okay, that's my cue to get coffee," I said under my breath, walking to the kitchen giving one last glance at the guys who seemed to be in an enthusiastic conversation.

My heart was bubbling with joy as I thought of the two close friends enjoying each other's company as I finished pouring a little cream in the cup.

Gerald's face was concentrating on the photo when I stood there holding his coffee.

Gerald cleared his throat. "Well, that's a first. I can't say I've ever experienced a spook before."

"Do you recognize the man on the porch?" Jessie asked.

"No, but my mom might know." Gerald's faced saddened.

"What's wrong?"

"I had to put her in the nursing home last week. It broke my heart. But I didn't have a choice."

"Is she okay?" I asked, concerned by Gerald's sudden change in demeanor.

Gerald took his uniform cap from his head and passed his hand over his thinning hair. "I'm not home all the time and I work some erratic hours on the road. Well, she almost burned the house down the other day by leaving something cooking on the stove. I've noticed her memory seems to be slipping more and more."

I placed my hand on Gerald's shoulder.

"She seems to remember the past but her day-to-day memory is getting worse."

"I'm sorry to hear that, Gerald. It must be hard on the both of you," Jessie said, clearing his throat.

We sat and contemplated a visit that afternoon.

CHAPTER 8

It was a cool, sunny day as we headed to the nursing home in Marksville. I knew both Jessie, and I were excited to find some answers about the old man in the picture.

As we pulled into the front parking lot, I was mesmerized by the place and by how huge it was. When we entered we stood eyeing each of the hallways and noticed there were different sections like a hospital. In fact, it was quite impressive. The hallways were large and carpeted with wonderful bright paintings lining the walls. Each room was either single or double occupancy with their own televisions. We passed a refreshment station and grabbed some free coffee before making our way deep into the jungle of the never-ending hallways. We were thankful Gerald had given us clear instructions on how to find his mom.

It was quiet as we entered her room to find a frail, petite woman with short white hair and glasses sitting in a comfy-looking recliner and reading a book. The room was small with little furniture and had its own bathroom and closet.

"Mrs. Juneau?" I asked.

"Yes," she said, raising her head from her book.

"Hi, I'm Sarah and this is Jessie. We are friends of Gerald. He said it would be all right for us to stop by and visit with you today."

The corner of her mouth lifted, and a sparkle came to her eyes.

"I love the company. Come sit on the bed next to me."

She looked at Jessie intently. "Don't I know you?"

"Yes, ma'am. I used to work with Gerald. I've been to your house for supper a time or two."

She gave a slight smile, and it was obvious she was trying to register Jessie's comment and place him in her memory.

"Yes, I remember. It's good to see you. How are your folks?"

"They passed away years ago."

"I'm sorry to hear that. I knew them. They lived across the bayou from Mr. Andrew."

"That's why we are here. Would you recognize the man on the porch of this house?" I asked, handing her the picture along with the magnifying glass I'd brought from home.

She squinted her eyes, raising the photo and magnifier closer to her face. "I don't know that lady there." She pointed. "But the man definitely looks like old man Andrew."

"Do you know if he built that house?"

"Oh no, that house was built back in the eighteen-hundreds. My mom and dad would have known who built that house."

She paused, and I watched as the corners of her mouth turned up. "I'm no spring chicken, but if I remember correctly, that man moved into the house in the early nineteen-hundreds." She laid the picture on her lap. "He was a handsome man." She giggled as her cheeks blushed. "He was the bad boy that every young girl wanted but was warned to stay away from. Tall, handsome and debonair, he was. That house had a lot of fancy parties when I was young. They would pack the front yard with Model T cars. Why, it was even rumored that Bonnie and Clyde attended several of his parties."

"Do you know if he was from around here?"

"No sugar, he was a foreigner from France or something. He would take long trips overseas and be gone for months at a time."

"Was he married or have any children?"

She giggles and her cheeks flushed again. "There wasn't a girl on the bayou didn't want to marry that man, but I don't think he ever married."

She handed me the picture. "The man on that porch became more of a recluse after he got shot and couldn't walk anymore."

My mouth fell open in complete shock. "He was shot? What happened?"

"It was rumored that when he got back from one of his overseas trips, someone broke into his house and shot up the place with a machine gun. He was hit by one of those stray bullets. They ransacked the place from top to bottom. Police said it was an armed robbery gone bad."

"Did they catch the shooter?" Jessie asked.

"No, whoever it was, done their damage, and got out of town. I never heard if they ever arrested anyone."

I looked at Jessie with eyes wide.

"His party days were over after that. The only movement there was a nurse living with him, taking care of things. He died a depressed, lonely old man. In fact, that lady in the picture could have been that nurse."

"Is that rumor, too?"

"What I know for a fact, is that long ago my girlfriend and I would pass on that road on our bicycles. I know for a fact, he had parties, and he had a lady living with him taking care of things after his accident." She paused as her cheeks became rosy, "And I remember how suave and debonair he was," she said with an expression of a schoolgirl with a hidden fantasy. "I never told my mom and dad, but one day my girlfriend and I got up the nerve to visit him. I get the chill bumps just thinking about it." She rubbed her arms.

"Now the rumors about that man run as long as my arm. It was rumored about Bonnie and Clyde, gangsters, speaking four languages fluently, hidden treasure or money from a mafia robbery being in that house, that's all hearsay." She paused. "Of course, with some rumors, there is almost always also a bit of truth."

Jessie cleared his throat and swallowed hard. "Did you say mafia?"

"Yes, he was known to be in the mafia. And the rumor was, he stole something of great value from another mafia family and brought it here to Louisiana from overseas and then hid it in the house he lived in. Not sure if it was money, jewels, or gold. Just remember, it was a fantastic tale in my day. Andrew was so kind and polite. I can't imagine him being a bad boy. But it makes sense that the mafia would come shoot up the place looking for their money, or whatever it was," she said with a faraway, wistful look.

"My God, the mystery of that house continues to build," I whispered under my breath.

Jessie reached over and squeezed my hand.

Mrs. Juneau smiled and asked, "Did you say you are friends with my son?"

"Yes, ma'am. I worked with your son in the police department."

"Oh, you look familiar. You know you two make a nice couple. Does Gerald know you came to visit?"

"Yes, ma'am, he knows."

"Well, okay, it was nice to meet you," she said, picking up her book to read again.

We took her comment as a sign to go.

On the way to the entrance, Jessie excused himself, leaving me looking at the pictures in the hallway.

Suddenly, chills ran down my body. I grabbed my arms in a hug to get the feeling of dread under control.

In the glass reflection of the picture, I saw a man peering at me from around the corner.

My body shook as I recognized the fat slob from the restaurant, slash bar we had dinner at, that evening over a month ago. And the same man that was watching me at the courthouse days ago.

Why was he everywhere I went, and what the hell did he want?

Anger replaced the dread and fear as I turned towards him, to find him just inches from me.

Startled, I gasped as he walked closer. I inched my back up against the wall. He leaned in on me, supporting his weight with his arm. I held my breath and clenched my fist, waiting for a chance to smack him.

"So, we meet again. How convenient for me that you've been left unattended, again. This is my lucky day," he whispered, getting close to my ear.

Shaking, I raised my hand to push against his chest to put distance between us as I turned my face and tried not to inhale the stale smell of beer and bad breath.

He was obviously an alcoholic since it was only four in the afternoon and he smelled like a lush.

I searched the hall for help, but saw no one. What would I do?

He was so fat and solid I couldn't budge his body away from me. Out of the corner of my eye, I saw his slow descent towards my face again. Pressing firmly against the wall with my face turned, I waited.

In the background, I could hear a toilet flush from the bathroom.

I could feel my heart racing and my breath started coming in quick bursts. My legs became weak, and I worried I might collapse to the floor as I anticipated his dreaded breath upon my face.

With my fist clenched, I opened my eyes to give a swing only to find empty space.

My eyes frantically searched to the right and then to the left and found no one.

In the distance, I heard the water running in the men's bathroom. I wondered if he escaped my punch by hiding in there.

I drug my heavy legs towards the bathroom. Seconds from pushing on the door, Jessie walked out.

"Are you all right? You're looking kind of pale. Do you need to sit down?"

"I, I. Is there someone else in the bathroom with you?"

"No, why?"

I wasn't sure if what just happened was real or not. How could he have disappeared so fast?

"Yes, I need to sit down a minute."

Jessie took my elbow and walked me to some nearby chairs in the same area. "Are you going to tell me what happened? Or are we going to play twenty questions?"

"I saw that man again." Looking at Jessie, I could tell he was clueless about what I was talking about.

"You remember the man from the bar and the courthouse?"

"Ah, yes."

"He's here. I saw him."

"Did he hurt you? I'll kill that son-of-a-bitch," Jessie sneered as I watched his face flush and his body tense up.

I grabbed Jessie's arm, keeping him from standing.

"No, I'm okay. He's, he's gone."

"What happened?"

"He just appeared and… and was gone before I could… before I knew it."

Since I wasn't hurt, I saw no point in going into greater detail about the close encounter with the man. I just wanted to be rid of the awful experience and his awful stale odor.

"Let's just go, all right?"

It was a quiet ride back to the house as we both seemed to be letting the events of the day sink in.

The story Mrs. Juneau told fascinated me, but it was hard to concentrate on that when I had the need for a long hot shower when I got back to rid myself of the stench of that awful man.

CHAPTER 9

By late afternoon, as we sat at the kitchen table eating, Jessie stopped in the middle of dinner and looked at me with a somber look.

"Hun, I really need to discuss something with you."

"Okay," I said, curious as to the worried look on his face.

"I don't want you going shopping or anything without me. Understand?"

"Is this about what happened at the nursing home?"

"Of course it is, Sarah. I know you're not telling me everything that happened to you today."

"I, I…" Stammering, my head fell to my chest, ashamed that he knew I was holding back on the events at the nursing home with that stranger.

"Sarah, you can't play with fire and not get burned. This man is dangerous. If he has the audacity to confront you in a public place like the bar, courthouse, and the nursing home in broad daylight, then he has no fear. A person with no fear is dangerous beyond belief."

"But… I'm not hurt."

"Not this time, but the fear I saw on your face was undeniable," Jessie said, angrily slamming his fist on the table.

"Yes, he scared me, just like you're scaring me now."

Jessie stepped towards me, pulling me up from my chair and embracing me tightly. With our foreheads touching, he continued, "I'm sorry, boo. It's not my intention to scare you. I just… I feel like my hands are tied behind my back. I would never forgive myself if something happened to you."

"Is that why you were talking to Gerald at the end of the driveway this afternoon?"

"You saw that?"

"Well, yeah. When I got out of the shower, I couldn't find you. When I looked outside, there the two of you were."

Jessie cleared his throat. "Sit."

I sat wondering what was so serious in his actions. "Why didn't he come in for coffee?"

Jessie sat in his chair and took my hand.

My body shivered, bringing about fear. "Please don't tell me Hank was caught at the end of the driveway again?"

"No. But Gerald found someone else pulled into the driveway that was a stranger. But again, this is a dead-end road; it's possible he was just turning around using our driveway."

Fear gripped my chest like a vise, making my breath catch in my chest. It had to be the same man. He followed us home, and now he knew where I lived.

"Since we just got back from our visit with Mrs. Juneau, I figured it was the stranger from the nursing home who followed us back." Jessie seemed to pause in thought. "Did this man who approached you have sandy colored curly hair and was he dressed in old clothes that looked like they were two sizes too small?"

"I, uh, I'm not sure what color hair he had, he always has on a dull gray cap. But yes, he dresses like a slob. He's overweight with a beer belly and is a little taller than me. Did Gerald get the man's name?"

"No, he brushed it off as just someone turning around. But that is who he described."

"I guess we should have talked to Gerald about this stranger at the nursing home as soon as it happened?"

"Yeah, we should have."

This info sat in my stomach like a brick. "This means that awful man knows where I live."

"Don't worry, boo, I'm here."

That was when a flashback of everything that had happened in the house ran through my mind like a raging river. The break-ins, Hank shooting Jessie, the emergency room visit due to infection. I couldn't help but have a premonition of impending doom. Maybe it was because these flashbacks kept coming to me or was it because Jessie almost died, and the thought of something happening to him was just overwhelming. It felt like all this crap with this house was about to get worse again before it got better.

"I don't want to talk about this anymore. Leave the dishes, we need some miracle time," I said, standing.

Jessie grinned with one eyebrow lifted.

I grabbed his hand, and we left out the back door to the boat dock. We crossed the bayou just in time to watch Jessie's parents' celestial bodies appear at the end of the dock. It never failed to help me put things in a better perspective watching them.

Things like that didn't just happen by accident. I couldn't help but think there is a true purpose in life. Whether good or bad in nature, the purpose always has a learning quality to it. I have learned so much since my life changed from my New York days to the Bayou days. I smiled because even though I dreaded what I saw with my eyes; I knew in the background in another dimension we were watched, loved, and guided in our purpose on earth.

Lying in bed next to Jessie that night, I wondered if maybe with all the events and feelings of dread in the days ahead, wasn't a warning that maybe I would suffer a significant loss. Maybe my time on earth was ending, and I needed to prepare for it, but how?

During the night I awoke to a feeling of something cold and wet under me. I sat up to find blood all over the sheets. My eyes followed the blood to the floor. As though I was gliding on air, I followed the blood trail to the hidden door in the wall. I pushed on the panel and opened the door to follow the blood inside. Whose blood was this, and why was there so much of it? Was someone hurt?

I awoke with gentle arms guiding me back to bed. "It's okay, sweetheart. You're sleepwalking," Jessie's soft voice calmly announced.

I turned to look at Jessie as my body shook in fear and I pulled him close to me. "I'm scared," I whispered.

"It's okay, let's get back to bed and we'll talk about it tomorrow."

Jessie pulled the sheet over me and climbed in bed and cuddled me until I drifted off to sleep.

CHAPTER 10

I felt Jessie's presence on the side of the bed along with the strong, rich aroma of coffee rousing me. Yawning, I turned and whispered good morning to Jessie as I sat up and he handed me the hot cup.

Waiting for the caffeine to kick in I stared into space, hoping Jessie wouldn't bring up last night's sleepwalking episode until my brain was firing on all cylinders.

The silence between us was uncomfortable. I looked at him. His handsome face always sent butterflies to my stomach. This morning his flawless face had an unusual crease in his forehead. Was that a worry line, I wondered.

Jessie lifted his head and looked me straight in the eyes. The deep concern in his hazel eyes made my heart expand with love.

"I love you, Sarah," was all he said in a soft, loving tone.

My heart leaped in my chest as I put my hand on his knee, "I love you too."

He reached for my hand and clasped it firmly. "Last night was not the first time I caught you sleepwalking, is it?"

I felt my eyes water up, threatening to spill over. "No." My heart ached inside because he caught me in a lie. Why did I come up with a fabricated story of a mouse? I should have told him I was dreaming.

"Why didn't you tell me you sleepwalk?" He asked gently.

"Because I've never done that before until now, and it scared me."

"What were you dreaming about?"

"Honestly... I was dreaming of blood, a lot of blood everywhere. It trailed off into the hidden wall."

"Is that all?"

"Yeah, you always wake me before I find where all the blood is coming from."

Jessie let go of my hand and looked down at his empty cup. "Is there anything else you haven't told me?"

"Well, uh," I paused. "Yeah. I found something the other day when you went to the store," I said timidly, hoping he wouldn't be mad.

"What?" Jessie asked.

"I'll show you." I put my cup down on the side table and scooted off the bed on Jessie's side and went to the hidden panel in the wall.

"Well, are you coming?" I said as I waited for him to get up and follow me.

I made my way inside the narrow, dark corridor and showed him my first find, the peephole. "Follow me, there's more." Then I continued up the ladder to the secret room with Jessie behind me. My face heated up when I realized I was still in my short nightshirt, exposing my butt to the man I loved. Well, at least I have on my fancy black lace underwear, I thought, clearing my throat, trying not to giggle.

Jessie stood beside me as I showed him the latch that opened the hidden wall to the upstairs hallway.

He walked past me through the wall to the hallway, opening and closing the wall and inspecting it closely. He stood scratching his head with a look of amazement. "Whoever built this was super smart. You would never guess this was here, huh?"

Jessie paused, running his fingers through his thick brown hair. "Why did that man need such a place unless he had something to hide? Or was he hiding from someone?"

"Is there a way to open it from the hallway?" I asked, curious, and wondering if the rumor of this man being in the French Mafia was true. That would explain so much about the house.

"Stay there while I close the wall and see if I can find a way in."

I stood there motionless, listening through the wall at Jessie's movements. Finally, I heard a click, and the wall opened.

"It's just like the wall in your bedroom, just push here and it opens."

"I never would have figured that out," I said, amazed.

We both stopped when we heard footsteps on the front porch and a knock at the door.

I gasped. "I'm not dressed," I nervously whispered.

Jessie chuckled and pushed on the wall. "Go back through here to the bedroom and get dressed. I'll get the door." Jessie reached over and slapped my butt, leaning in to whisper in my ear. "That sure is some fancy drawers for the swamp."

"Drawers?" I asked, dumbfounded. "Oh, panties," I said, my face feeling like a hot poker stick as I shyly smiled at Jessie.

He gave me an evil grin and a wink and walked down the steps.

Hurrying to dress, I could hear the usual voices of friendship in the living room.

Passing by the living room, I swept my long hair over my shoulder and asked, "Coffee?"

"No, not today, Sarah. I only have a minute. Come sit."

Dread filled my heart and my body responded as if I had heavy weights attached to my ankles. He always had coffee. He makes time for coffee. What could be more important than coffee?

"I just wanted to let you know I have no leads on the black truck or the driver from the other day, I'm sorry to say."

I let out a sigh. "Oh, I thought you had bad news."

Gerald's lips curled up slightly. "No, not today. In fact, I have excellent news."

"Really?"

"Yes. They pushed up the trial date and Hank will appear before the judge day after tomorrow. So you and Jessie need to be there around nine that morning."

"Thank God, it will be so nice when all this Hank business will be over and done with and I won't have him to worry about," I paused. "One attempted murderer out the way and now just a stalker to worry about."

"I'm sorry that I don't have better news about the stranger, I caught in your driveway, Sarah," Gerald said with big puppy dog eyes looking at me.

"It's okay. He may not show up again and I've been given strict instructions not to leave Jessie's side, not even to go grocery shopping," I announced, cocking my head towards Jessie with my eyebrows arched.

"That's right and don't you forget it," Jessie replied with a twinkle in his eyes. "What about that crooked lawyer, Brian Thibodaux?" he asked.

Gerald removed his cap, scratched his head, then replaced his cap. "I still have nothing concrete to arrest him on. I'm just glad you're keeping your distance from him. But I tell you what, every dog has his day and as long as I'm Sheriff I'll be keeping my eye on him. You can count on that."

Gerald stood to leave, then turned around. "Mom enjoyed your visit the other day," he chuckled. "She can't remember why you were there, but she said I had some nice friends."

"It was a joy to meet her. She gave us some interesting tips about the old man."

"I'd like to hear about that one day, but I am pressed for time." Gerald turned and walked out the door with a backward glance.

Jessie and I sat there in the quiet for a minute. "So..." I paused. "It sounded like you two had a lot to talk about until I came in. So what are you hiding? You wouldn't be holding important information from me, would you?"

Jessie's complexion took on a pink hue, as if he got caught with his hand in the cookie jar. "No, of course not." Jessie pulled me up from the couch and hugged me tightly. "I don't know what I would do without you. You know I would lay down my life for you, right?"

I pushed him back with a questioning look. "What's wrong with you? Why are you talking like that? I know you love me and would take a bullet for me." I paused, wondering what he was planning. Something inside didn't sit right, but I couldn't put my finger on it.

CHAPTER 11

The next morning, after a dreamless night, I was thankful for our usual morning ritual together.

After, I started cleaning and examining the rooms upstairs while Jessie went outside to continue painting. I paid close attention to anything out of the ordinary and pushed and kicked the walls for another possible hidden passageway, but found nothing out of the ordinary. But of course, I didn't have Jessie's eagle eyes to help me.

Exhausted and dirty after dusting and cleaning the floors, replacing old curtains, and stripping the bed sheets to be washed, I finally made my way to the third bedroom. I came across what looked like a ladder in the closet leading to a covered square in the ceiling. With my hands on my hips, looking up, I blew a loose strand of hair from my face and decided it was the entrance to the attic.

Too tired to investigate, I made my way downstairs for a quick sandwich with Jessie and to put a load of sheets in the washing machine.

"Are you finished cleaning upstairs?" Jessie asked, wiping the crumbs from the corner of his mouth.

"Almost," I replied, taking a sip of some iced tea. "I found the entrance to the attic."

"That's great. I bet they have some interesting things up there."

I giggled. "I was thinking the same thing."

"Well, how about we finish up here and check it out?"

"You read my mind, boo."

It wasn't twenty minutes later before Jessie was removing the cover of the entrance to the attic. I backed away, covering my nose and mouth with my tee-shirt as a light cloud of dust fell to the floor.

"Give me your hand and I will help you up the ladder."

With his strength, he pulled me up, and we stood motionless while our eyes adjusted to the darkness of the attic.

The only light that filtered in was at one end of the attic through a small stained glass window.

There was an overpowering musty smell in the air. I was finding it hard to breathe. I had this overwhelming feeling of claustrophobia from the darkness, heat, and the closeness of the roof.

My body vibrated with fear, and I moved closer to Jessie. Something didn't feel right up here, and I was ready to leave.

I pulled on Jessie's arm. "Can we go back downstairs?"

"Hold on a minute. Let me see if I can find a light switch or something."

Jessie walked away from me leaving me alone in the dark as my heart beat fast and my respiration started coming in short, quick shallow breaths. I was feeling overwhelmed and knew if I didn't get out of there, an anxiety attack would develop.

I heard a click and a small light came on. "There we go," Jessie said in a relieved tone.

Jessie saw my face and raced to my side. "It's okay, boo, I'm here," he said, pulling me close and lightly kissing my forehead.

Once my breathing got back to normal, I loosened my grip, and we both started looking around, finding boxes and old lamps bunched together in one spot. At the far end of the attic, under a half-moon glass window, I saw an old wheelchair. I presumed it was the same chair that was in the ghost photo of the old man.

I pointed to the wheelchair. "Why would someone keep such an old relic as that?"

Jessie was rummaging through the boxes and shrugged his shoulders, saying, "Why would anyone keep any of this old junk? I'm not an expert on antiques, but to me, there isn't anything worth salvaging."

"I agree. Now can we go back downstairs?"

Jessie's head jerked around to me. "You really are uncomfortable up here, aren't you?"

"Yes, something doesn't feel right," I said as a cool breeze hit my body, giving me a chill from my head to my toe. "You can stay up here, but I have to leave," I announced, as I started my descent down the ladder.

"I'm coming, I'm coming," I heard as I took in a deep breath of clean air when my foot hit the floor, relieved to be out of that attic.

"Be sure and close that lid," I demanded.

He chuckled. "Are you afraid someone will get you from the attic?"

"You never know. This old house has one secret after another. I don't want to take any chances."

"Yes, dear." Jessie smiled as he carefully pulled the lid over the hole.

"I don't know about you, but I need some fresh air," I said, not waiting for him to follow. All I knew was I needed to get out of there.

"Sounds good to me. Let me show you how much I've completed on the house."

After inhaling some fresh air on the porch, Jessie took my hand and led me several yards across the front lawn to get a view of the house.

I gasped as my jaw dropped as I looked at the front of the house in complete awe and joy.

"Jessie! It looks like a different house from the first day I got here." The paint was fresh and white and the grey shutters were painted and re-hung and with the new curtains in the window it looked like a Thomas Kincaid painting.

"Oh, Jessie!" I squealed and jumped upon him, wrapping my legs around his waist, squeezing him tight and giving him one kiss after another all over his face.

He laughed. "I've never seen you this happy before."

I slid down his body, standing next to him admiring his wonderful handy work and wished the inside of the house felt as good as the outside looked. Deep down inside I knew something was not right with the house, no matter how great it looked on the outside.

"Jessie, you're wonderful."

"I know."

I laughed and leaned my head on his chest. "I know it took a while for you to complete, after the gunshot and all, but you did an excellent job. No wonder my Aunt hired you to help around here."

After a long day of cleaning and working outside, we had a leisurely dinner and went to bed early.

"Are you ready for tomorrow, boo?"

"Not really, but the sooner we get this behind us the better."

"I agree."

Jessie pulled me close and wrapped his arms around me while I snuggled into him. His aroma after a hot shower made me want to stay in his arms forever. I couldn't wait for the next chapter of our lives to begin.

CHAPTER 12

Morning came too early. I sat on the front porch with knots in my stomach waiting for Jessie to make sure the back door was locked and the outside security cameras were working properly.

I was so nervous about seeing Hank face to face again after he shot Jessie trying to kill me. But a part of me was relieved to know that asshole would finally get what was coming to him. I really hoped they would lock him up for many years to come.

"Let's go, sweetheart," Jessie said, extending his hand to me.

His warm, loving touch calmed my soul as we made our way to the car.

"Sarah, I don't want you to worry, but it is possible he will plead guilty like Gerald said and they may release him to go back to New York. Will you have a problem with that?"

"Damn, Jessie, I should ask you that. You're the one who got shot."

His pearly white teeth shone bright like a sunny day. "As long as that son-of-a-bitch is gone, whether in jail or out of the state of Louisiana, I'll be happy."

"I agree."

The courthouse parking lot was packed, and we had to park a block away.

"Guess they're having court today," Jessie teased.

Gerald was already waiting for us outside the courtroom, pacing like an expectant father outside a delivery room.

"I couldn't get in touch with you. They upped the time. And he is before the judge right now."

"Oh my, do I need to be in there?" I asked, my legs feeling like jelly.

"No, go sit down and I'll check to see what's going on."

My body shook uncontrollably as I watched the double doors to the courtroom, expecting the worst possible outcome.

Jessie reached over and put his hand on mine. I looked up at his face and caught a movement down the hall.

Oh no, that's all I need, I said to myself as I watched that scumbag lawyer slowly making his way towards me. A grin came across his face as he recognized me.

Jessie saw the look on my face and then turned to see what I was looking at.

Brian's smile faded from his face and he stopped short, then slowly did a quick turn and walked away.

"It's Brian Thibodeaux." I sighed in relief when he changed direction.

I could feel Jessie's hand tense up and squeeze my hand.

"You better run, you snake," Jessie growled under his breath.

The courtroom door opened, and I jumped. Thank God it was Gerald.

The sheriff quickly made his way to us and sat next to me. He leaned in and whispered, "It's over."

We both sat there motionless with shock.

"What?" Was all I could manage to say.

Gerald passed a hand over his face.

I knew by now that was a sign of something bad.

"He pled guilty and was given credit for time served. The judge has ordered him out of the state of Louisiana."

"You mean that asshole doesn't have to pay for shooting me?" Jessie asked as the muscles in his jaw tightened.

"He has one of the best lawyers' money can buy. But on a wonderful note, they have ordered him to pay all your medical bills and report to New York to see a Probation Officer. He will be on probation for years to come. So, he technically didn't get away with anything," Gerald announced with pride.

"I was hoping he had to do more time, but as long as he is going back to New York and far away from us, I'm happy."

"You're right, sweetheart. As long as he doesn't show his sorry face around here again, that's good enough for me."

The doors opened and people started flowing out. My eyes locked on Hank as he walked out with an older gray-haired man in an expensive suit. They both seemed to walk with a look of pride and smugness.

His eyes caught mine, and I watched the corner of his mouth raise, which felt like a dagger to my heart. I could feel the heat of anger rise in my face as my eyes shot fire darts from hell at him. I held myself down as everything within me wanted to jump up and scratch his eyes out. Jessie's arm came around my shoulder tightly, as if he knew what was going on in my mind. Or was he showing possession of me in an I have her and you don't kind of way? It didn't matter to me why he held me tight; I was just glad he did.

As the people dispersed and Gerald took his leave, we were left sitting there somberly as though the wind had been knocked out of our sails. A piece of the puzzle was finally solved, leaving me wondering what this commotion was all about in the first place. Oh yeah, a stupid rumor of hidden treasure left in my house by a French gangster in the eighteen-hundreds.

I started to giggle.

Jessie looked at me as though I'd lost my mind. "What's so funny?"

I giggled even more until I was in full laughter with tears running down my cheeks.

Jessie's smile turned to laughter as we both laughed. "What is it?" he asked as he tried to catch his breath.

"It's… it's because of a stupid rumor." I laughed and snorted as my face went red and the surrounding people smiled and laugh along with us.

"What rumor?" Jessie laughed harder.

I smacked my knee, heaving with laughter as I heard others laughing. The contagious mirth echoed down the hall as more and more people joined in.

The courtroom door opened and a security guard came out. "Court is in session, stop this noise immediately," he said.

After standing there a minute, it was obvious he wanted to laugh, too, as he witnessed the spread of laughter in the halls. But he dared not be seen to be less than stern and serious, as his job demanded. He almost succeeded, but failed.

I straightened up for a moment, taking control of myself, only to lose it again a mere three seconds later. Jessie got me up, and we slowly made our way down the hall. I looked back to see the guard trying to stop laughing before entering the courtroom.

The rest of the people in the hallway were coming around, wiping tears from their eyes and breathing slow and deep.

By the time we made it outside into the bright sunshine, Jessie had settled down and gave me a puzzled look.

"All of this commotion with Hank was just over a simple rumor of hidden treasure in the house from a few hundred-year-old French mobster," I said.

Jessie grinned. "You're right, it sounds absurd." We walked a few more steps, then stopped. "You know; we are at the courthouse. We can go finish our investigation of the records, since we're here."

I thought about it a minute, then agreed. What were the odds that pervert would be in there again?

The place was empty and quiet as we made our way back to the section where land sales records were stored. I looked around, confident there was no one spying on us.

After about thirty minutes of searching, we finally came across an entry in a ledger showing the transfer of my land from one person to another. It was dull and yellowed with age, and some parts were illegible. But it looked like that parcel of land was once owned by the Tunica Biloxi Indians and had been donated to someone with the last name that I couldn't make out. There was also a permit to build a small house listed. Further down it showed the sale of the land to an Andrew St. Pierre and then another permit to build onto that same house. This all started back in the early nineteen-hundreds, just like Gerald's mom said.

We searched more, but found nothing else of interest except the sale to my Aunt.

I came away from our search of the house disappointed. There were no new blueprints to be found to see if there were any other hidden rooms. My heart sank in my chest because I had expected and hoped for more. What is a name? Andrew St. Pierre could be anyone.

CHAPTER 13

After a stressful day, the night came quickly. As I lay in Jessie's arms, listening to his rhythmic breathing, my mind continued to circle around and around of the day's events.

Who was this mobster, and why did my aunt buy his house? It had been over a month since we found the body in the basement, so why hadn't anyone contacted us? Surely there should be some kind of follow-up. Most of all, what were Gerald and Jessie always talking about that they felt the need to stop whenever I came into the room?

When I finally went to sleep, my nightmare started all over again. This time I noticed blood on my hands and night-shirt as I set my foot on the floor to follow the blood trail to the wall. My feet were trying to touch the floor, but I couldn't reach it. That's when I realized firm hands were grabbing me and I woke up to Jessie trying to get me to lie down.

"There's blood, I have to see who got hurt. Let me go," I argued.

Jessie pulled me close and whispered, "It's okay. You're safe and sound. You're only dreaming." He sighed. "I promise things will look better tomorrow."

With his soothing words, I fell off into the dream world one more time.

When I awoke again, the sun was shining through the window and Jessie was still holding me close. I looked at the clock to see that it was early, and instead of going back to sleep, I went ahead and made coffee for Jessie.

As I made our special brew, I couldn't help but wonder why I'd had so much blood on me. Hopefully, Hank would go back to New York and it wasn't his blood all over me. I knew in my heart that if he set foot in this house again, I would hurt him. Badly.

"He's got another thing coming if he thinks he is going to come up in my house shooting a gun again. I'll put him six feet under. I'll protect what's mine. I'll…"

Jessie came up behind me and asked, "Who are you going to kill?"

"Oh, I was just thinking out loud."

"Obviously," he said as he took the cup of steaming hot coffee that I offered him.

"It's a cool morning. Let's go sit on the back porch."

As we settled onto the porch swing, I looked at him and told him about my dream. "I had blood all over me in my dream and I was wondering if maybe I killed Hank. And then was thinking if he came back to my house with a gun, I was going to put him six feet under."

Jessie chuckled. "Remind me not to get you angry."

I hit his leg. "Don't be silly. I wouldn't hurt you… unless." I paused to try to come up with something humorous to make the conversation less morbid. "Unless you come at me with a gun." I paused. "Jessie? Please let me go see where the blood leads to, the next time I go sleepwalking around? If there is a next time?"

Jessie glared at me intently. "Are you sure you want to know where the blood leads to and who may be bleeding?"

I thought about it for a minute. "Well, yeah, I guess. I figure I'm having these dreams like a premonition. So I think I need to know."

"You may be right, boo. I tell you what, next time you start sleepwalking I will just follow you so you don't get hurt. Is that okay with you?"

"That sounds like a plan."

Since the cool weather was coming in Jessie decided it would be a good time to winterize the house pipes, so a quick trip to the hardware store was first on our list for the day.

As we picked up the supplies my heart felt light. I was in love, and with Hank out of the way, I felt this heavy energy leave me.

I hummed and strolling around, looking at things and imagining my house with this, that, and the other thing when I accidentally backed into someone.

"Oh, excuse me," I offered as I turned to see the same fat slob that had been harassing me for the past several weeks.

"Funny meeting you here, pretty little Miss." He leaned in and smelled the air near my ear. "Mm, mm good, you smell good enough to eat."

I turned to leave, and he clutched my arm tightly. He whispered, "I'm watching you."

"You're hurting me, you... you." I started to scream when he released my arm with a push and quickly walked around the corner of the aisle.

With my heart racing and my body shaking, I backed up, making sure he didn't come back. Watching over my shoulder, I tried to quickly find Jessie. Two aisles over I found him talking to Mary, the cashier.

He turned and looked at me. "What's wrong? You look like you've seen a ghost."

"He's here," I managed to squeak out with what little strength I had left.

Jessie immediately dropped his items and ran down each aisle, looking for my tormentor. He came back to my side, shaking his head. "I don't see anyone here. Are you sure it was him?"

"How can you question me like this? Seems like you don't believe me." I pulled the sleeve of my shirt up and showed him where the man had forcefully grabbed my arm.

"Does this look fake to you?" I asked with tears threatening to spill over onto my face.

Jessie came up to me and held me close. "I'm sorry, honey. I didn't mean to say I didn't believe you. It's just..."

I pushed away from him. "It's just what?"

He took his cap from his head and combed his thick, dark hair back.

He cleared his throat. "It's just that I'm right here and I still can't seem to keep you safe. Unless I glue you to my side with some of this strong glue." He picked up a tube of bonding cement from the floor. "I'm afraid I might slip up and something awful will happen."

He looked like a lost puppy with sad eyes, and his lips slightly tilted down.

"He seems to maneuver well in public places without me seeing him."

I looked to Mary, who had put her hand to her mouth, her eyes wide with fear.

"I'm so sorry, Sarah and Jessie, I didn't mean to eavesdrop. I had no idea someone was harassing you like that."

"It's okay, Mary. Every dog has his day, and his day is about up." I smiled, trying to ease the fear I saw in her eyes.

"So you've seen him before?" she asked.

"Yes, at the nursing home, the courthouse, at the bar, and now, here. And someone saw him hanging around my driveway."

"Oh dear, did you contact the Sheriff's department?"

"Yes, of course, we did. We just don't know who he is or how far he will go with his harassment."

"If there is anything I can do, please let me know," Mary said, walking to the front of the store.

Jessie finished picking up the items he had dropped, and we followed Mary to the front to check out, as I continuously looked over my shoulder as nonchalantly as possible.

My body was starting to ache around my shoulders, and I tried to relax. I'd gone from light and free to tense and scared in just a matter of seconds. I guess when a psychopath is following you around everywhere, you just can't let your guard down. I had to wonder, though, if he was in the store already, or did he just happen to be at all those places I saw him. Could he really be tracking my every movement? He said he had been watching me...

I jumped when Jessie touched my arm. "What? Did you say something?"

"I said we're here."

"Oh, okay." I looked around to see we were home already. I didn't even remember checking out at the store or the ride home. I really needed to pay more attention, instead of worrying to the point of not knowing where I was. That could prove to be a dangerous distraction.

"I'll get busy wrapping the pipes. If you're up to it, can you start a gumbo? The weather is getting cooler every day." He gazed at me intently. "You do remember how to fix a gumbo like I showed you, right?"

"Of course I do. I can manage in the kitchen," I paused, "until you're finished."

"It won't take me long and I'll come back to help," Jessie said as he closed the door to the car with bundles of supplies under his arm.

The gumbo was well underway when Jessie made his way back into the house. After careful inspection of the pot and a taste test, he lowered the heat then grabbed my hand. "Let's make our way across the bayou while this simmers."

The spiritual encounter was always a wonderful distraction to what was going on in my life.

Like clockwork, Jessie's parents appeared to us as we lounged in front of the house.

My mouth dropped, and I gasped. Normally his parents would be there watching the sunset, but today, for the first time, they were facing us.

I grabbed Jessie's knee, gripped by disbelief. My eyes had to be playing tricks on me.

He immediately stood up and walked towards his parents. His parents held each other the way they always did. Jessie was inches from them when he reached out. Just as he was about to touch them, they vanished like wisps of smoke floating free.

I watched my love just standing there in shock. My heart went out to him. I could just imagine how much he missed them, and then to be so close and not be able to touch them. I bit my bottom lip in an effort to stop the tears which wanted to fall. I walked up behind him, circling my arms around his waist and pulling him close.

After a minute I asked, "Did they say anything?"

"No... they just stood there, and I felt this deep sense of love just wash over me. The love was so intense it penetrated my very soul."

"What do you think it meant?"

"I don't know, but I feel like they were telling me that no matter what life throws at me they will be with me, guiding me and giving me strength."

He turned to look at me. "Sarah, I love you so much," he said, cupping my face.

Something didn't feel right. Fear vibrated through me like electricity. "What's wrong?" I whispered with dread in my heart.

"I have this feeling something is about to happen and I want you to know we can get through this together. I'm will not leave your side and I will help you no matter the cost."

Jessie firmly grabbed my shoulders. "Remember this." He paused. "No matter what you see before you or around you, you must handle all things from the strength within."

"I'm not sure I understand what you're saying; you're scaring me."

He pulled me close and hugged me so tight the air in my lungs expelled.

"Everything I do, I do because I love you," he whispered close to my ear.

I jerked away from him. "Have you lost your ever-loving-mind? You're not making any sense. What is wrong with you? I'm going back to the house. We still have gumbo on the stove," I said, marching towards the boat.

Jessie's action and words had my stomach in knots. And if he wasn't going to explain himself, then I would not let him pull me into this deep, depressing void of darkness with him. I needed to escape and escape now.

I walked several steps towards the boat, then whirled around. "Well, are you coming or not?" I said with all the attitude I could muster up.

"Yes, ma'am. I'm sorry, Sarah, I just wanted to…"

"I don't want to hear it. You're freaking me out, and I don't want to hear another word."

CHAPTER 14

We headed back to the house in silence. It seemed like the only noise was the ripple of the water against the boat and the small trolling motor. Now and then, you could hear something splash in the water and a frog croaking from on the banks of the Bayou.

I couldn't help but know in my heart that something was just over the horizon and I needed to prepare myself for it. The dreams were a dead giveaway. All that blood was not a good sign. I loved that he was affirming his love for me, but I guess I just didn't want to be warned of impending doom. It made it too real. It was moments like these that I wanted to turn back time and be back in New York in my comfy, cozy apartment overlooking the city and having a stable job and friends to hang around with. I wanted a nice, normal life without all this dark cloak and dagger excitement in the swamps.

After a couple of tweaks from Jessie's expert hand at cooking, the gumbo came out better than ever before. The silence between us was uneasy. No words were spoken at the table and no light touching. I wasn't sure what was worse, the scary way he talked to me earlier, with that deep underlying meaning that sent chills through me, or him giving me the silent treatment and avoiding me completely.

I longed for things to be normal again. I thought about it a moment and realized it had never been normal here. But there were brief periods of time that I treasured more than anything. I wanted my Jessie back, the lighthearted, loving man that made me feel safe and secure. I needed him to hold me and soothe my rambling mind before I had to be taken away in a straight-jacket.

I could hear my inner voice again, rambling on and on, wondering what Jessie knew that I didn't know. Were he and Gerald up to something? Is that why I would catch them talking in Cajun French whenever they were together? Had Hank really left Louisiana without a fight and without his beloved treasure? Why hadn't the FBI contacted me about the dead body in the basement? And most important of all, who was this stalker that ended up everywhere I went?

I felt a hand on my arm and I jumped. "I'm sorry, boo. I didn't mean to scare you." With his head down like a naughty little boy being scolded by his parents, Jessie said, "I didn't mean to make you more scared than you already are with all my talk. I just want to protect you, no matter what. You know that, right? I just wanted to reassure you that Gerald and I will find this guy that's harassing you and put him to justice. That's all."

"I know you love me. I guess what is scaring me is... I feel the same way. This guy is getting braver by the minute and I feel he is going to make a move soon. I just don't want my thoughts to be right."

Jessie stood from the table and pulled me up in his arms. "It will be okay, just don't leave my side. Understand?"

I hugged him around the waist tighter. "I'm not going anywhere."

He grabbed me up off the ground and planted a passionate kiss on me that curled my toes and started the fire going.

"Oh Jessie, how I wish we were married already."

"My little honey bun, I want that, too. As soon as your divorce is final, we will be man and wife and I'll show you some husbandly renovation."

"Renovation?" I asked with a puzzled look on my face.

"You saw how I replaced boards, painted, and made this old house look like new? Well, I'm going to do that to your body. You will be standing tall like a new woman once I get finished with you."

Giggles escaped my lips as I felt my face grow hot with embarrassment.

A knock on the door interrupted our thoughts.

I pushed away from Jessie's hold. "I'll get it."

My heart was light as I passed the mirror in the hallway and saw a big smile on my face. So, Sarah, this is what it looks like when you're in love. I couldn't help but watch my face flush again.

The knock came again. As I passed the staircase, I thought I saw movement out of the corner of my eye. It looked like that old wheelchair in the attic at the top of the staircase. When I turned to get a better look, there was nothing there. I stood there a minute, then answered the door.

"Hi, Gerald, good to see you. Would you like some gumbo before we put it up?"

"No, no, I just wanted to tell you my mom has asked to see you again. She said she remembers something about the old man that lived here."

"Oh, well, is it too late to go now?"

Gerald smiled. "If you don't go now, she may not remember what's on her mind."

Jessie walked into the room. "Where are we going?"

"Gerald said his mom remembers something about the old man that lived here and wants us to come by."

"Well, let's go. Are you coming with us, Gerald?"

"No, you go ahead."

As I grabbed my purse and keys I noticed out the corner of my eye Gerald give Jessie some kind of hand motion.

"What is up with you two? What are y'all cooking? I know something is up and I don't want any excuses," I demanded with my hand on my hip. "Well, who's going to spill the beans?" I asked.

Jessie spoke up. "He was motioning I had something on my shirt. It was just a piece of rice from the gumbo."

I didn't believe him for a minute. These two had secrets, and I knew it.

***

Supper dishes were just being picked up and tables being wiped down in the dining room as we walked down the hall looking for Gerald's mom's room. We entered to find her sitting alone.

"I've been waiting on y'all," she announced. "Have a seat on my bed," she pointed.

"Yes, ma'am. How are you feeling tonight, Ms. Juneau?" I asked, trying to be friendly.

"Uh, call me Geraldine." She shook her head. "I don't have time for small talk, young lady. I have to tell you this before I forget." She paused. "I wanted to tell you Mr. St. Pierre has a family."

My mouth fell open. "Family, here?" I asked.

"No... yes. She tried to buy the old house. But she didn't succeed."

"She? Who was this, exactly?"

"It was his sister."

"So there was competition trying to get the house along with Aunt Pauline."

"Yes, supposedly Andrew and his sister were inseparable until the alleged heist in France, after which Andrew fled to America. In time, she and her son found their way here. She was younger than him. I would think she is about my age... no younger."

"Would you happen to remember her name?" Jessie asked.

Geraldine hung her head for a moment. For a minute I thought she'd zoned out, and we would have to ask her again.

She lifted her head. I could see the wheels turning as her face suddenly brightened. "Daisy. That's it, her name is Daisy Wright."

She seemed so proud of herself I couldn't help but give her an ear to ear smile.

"Thanks, Mrs. Juneau. We sure appreciate your help."

"Call me Geraldine, I said."

"Okay, okay, Mrs. Geraldine."

"Did you know that Gerald was named after me?"

Jessie smiled, and I giggled. "No, we didn't know that."

"Well, now you know," she said with a huff and turned around.

I looked at Jessie and shrugged my shoulders. "I guess that's our cue to leave."

"Okay then, we'll be going." She never turned around, just lifted her hand at us by way of dismissal.

CHAPTER 15

On the way home, all we could do was bounce ideas off each other at what connection this Daisy Wright had in the house, or anything going on in the house. Was she connected to the perverted criminal that seemed to be everywhere I turned? Or was she even in the town of Marksville?

"So, I'm presuming Wright would be her married name, right?"

"Yeah, that would be my guess." Jessie paused. "We should have asked what her son's name was."

We got to the house and sat for a minute, digesting the additional information and wondering what it had to do with the mysteries this house held.

As we made our way up to the door Jessie put his hand out to stop me and whispered, "Stay here."

That's when I noticed the front door had a crack in it. Was someone in the house? It better not be Hank or I'd wring his sorry neck.

Jessie came back minutes later. "It's okay."

"Is anything missing?" I asked as I looked around.

"No, nothing looks disturbed," Jessie said, heading to the computer to look and see what the camera had picked up.

That's when I noticed the hall closet door under the stairs was not closed all the way. My hand started to shake as I reached for the doorknob. I forcefully pulled it open wide, cowering back and hoping there was nothing to see. The memories of that night last month and finding that hideous body still haunted me.

"Sarah, come see," Jessie yelled.

I shut the door and quickly made my way to Jessie's side. He glanced at me with a strange look on his face. "You have to see this."

He scooted over, giving me enough room to sit beside him on the chair, as I waited for him to replay whatever the camera picked up.

My breath caught in my throat as I watched the very faint, misty outline of an old man in a wheelchair come out the front door, then disappear into the corner of the front porch. I watched as the front door inched its way at a slow, steady pace, leaving about a one-inch gap.

"Aw, man. Not another ghost," I said, exasperated with it all.

"What I don't understand is... why now?" Jessie paused. "Why, after all these months, does this apparition show himself now?"

My hand automatically landed on Jessie's arm. "I don't know, honey. Nothing makes sense anymore. First, your parents turn and look at us, and now this old man appears right when we are feeling something is about to happen."

Jessie turned to me with his eyebrow cocked and a small grin.

"What?"

"You called me honey."

"Yeah, so?"

"It's very rare that you call me any pet names like that."

"Yeah, well, maybe this Cajun sweetness is rubbing off on me."

I shyly looked at him as the temperature seemed to rise several degrees and I felt the need for air. "Well, you are my honey, my love."

"That's right, and don't you forget it," Jessie replied, kissing my hand. "You know, I've had about enough excitement with the afterlife for a while," he said with a mischievous wink.

"Why don't you go take your shower 'honey' and I'll go clean up the kitchen and throw the scraps from dinner into the bayou." I winked back.

"Leave it for tomorrow," Jessie insisted.

"Don't be silly. I'll be back in a couple of minutes. I'm just going out the back door."

"Okay, let me know when you come back in."

"Deal," I said as I hurried to the kitchen to get rid of the leftover scraps from supper.

Jessie insisted we give the scraps to the fish in the bayou every day. He called it giving back to nature since we took so much from it.

I grabbed the old plastic whipped cream container full of leftover food and walked out the back door. The night was so chilly; I pulled my collar together, trying to keep the draft from going down my shirt.

That's when out of the corner of my eye I noticed a black shadow beside me. Before I understood what was happening, I felt and heard a thump on the side of my head and falling to the porch. The next thing I remembered was someone dragging me off the porch by my arms, as my body was thumping down the steps.

"No!" I screamed.

The black-figure dropped me to the ground like a brick and quickly came around, covering my mouth with a dark glove. The extreme force he used pushed my head into the dirt.

A low growl penetrated the silence. "If you want to live until tomorrow, you will keep quiet and do everything I say. Do you understand me?"

Fear gripped my body so tightly that everything in life stood still. I watched the figure get up from beside me and pull me up to my feet like I weighed nothing.

I was always told if someone kidnaps you, you must try to get away as soon as possible.

I tried to calm my racing heart as my eyes darted around to see where I could run when I made my move.

When he loosened his grip on my arms, I darted towards the steps away from him. I had just made the second step when he yanked on my shirt, causing me to fall forward on the porch as his hands groped for my ankles to keep me from moving forward.

With every ounce of strength I had, I turned and kicked him off me and tried running towards the front of the house, screaming and hoping Jessie wasn't in the shower yet.

He was too fast. When I was even with the fireplace, he tackled me to the ground with his heavy body, knocking the air out of my lungs.

Breathing heavily, I pulled and tugged on the bricks of the fireplace, trying to free myself from his grasp.

He stood up and grabbed me from the ground by my shoulders, slamming me against the bricks. My head hit hard, and I felt something warm run down the side of my face.

"I could kill you right now, you bitch," he said angrily next to my face.

He started to pull me away from the fireplace as I grasped at the bricks with what strength I could muster. A brick came loose, falling to the ground. There was something there, behind the brick. He yanked at my hair, pulling me back into his arms.

I lifted my legs, hoping I was too heavy for him, hoping that he would drop me, but he was too strong.

My breathing was coming in short, heavy gasps as I tried to yell out again.

The force of his hand on my face and around my waist made it hard to breathe.

Tears flowed down my cheek as I realized I had failed and this could be my last day on earth.

He carried me as effortlessly as a five-pound sack of potatoes as I tried to kick him and bite through his glove.

He made it to the edge of the yard into the tree line and my heart sank deep in my chest knowing this would end in disaster.

Since there was no sign of Jessie, I knew in my heart he was still showering and hadn't heard a thing. It would be maybe fifteen to twenty minutes before he realized I wasn't even there anymore.

In my mind, I resolved that as long as I had breath in my body I would fight, kick, and scream, since the alternative was probably death, anyway.

We went several yards into the woods by the house until he stopped and just dropped me to the ground.

I looked up to the shadowy figure and wondered what he was stopping for. So this is where I would die, just yards away from my house.

"Pick it up," he ordered.

I looked around but found nothing to pick up.

"I said pick it up," he demanded.

"It's freaking dark out here, what the hell do you want me to pick up?" I demanded back at him.

"Get up, bitch."

Was it another trap door leading to another underground basement? Were there dead bodies in there, too? Was I to be the next victim in his killing spree?

"Get in."

"No! You're out of your freaking mind if you think I'm going in that black hole."

I watched as he put his hand in his jacket pocket and pulled out something shiny. It was a knife. Not like any knife I had ever seen. It wasn't a straight blade but looked curved.

"Get in," he demanded sternly.

I stood my ground, not budging. I weakly rose to my feet, almost losing my balance because of the terrible pain in my head. My body felt worn out and weak, and I swayed with extreme exhaustion as nausea tried to erupt within me.

He forcefully pushed me out of the way, causing me to land on the ground with significant force. He then bent down and moved some twigs and leaves to reveal what looked like a trap door. He opened the latch and swung the trap door up and over on the ground opposite the hole.

My eyes widened as my mind went wild with questions. Had he dug this hole to dispose of my body?

I heard a low chuckle.

Shocked, I tried to search his face in the darkness.

"You act like I asked you nicely. I'm not asking, I'm demanding." He paused. "Get in before I slice your throat from here to here." He growled, making a gesture across his neck with the knife.

"I refuse to be buried alive out here in the swamps of Louisiana next door to my house," I said as I watched him raise his arm with the knife and I closed my eyes waiting for the impact.

It felt like slow motion as I waited for the knife to cut me. Those few seconds seemed like hours as I imagined him forcefully jabbing the knife into my body and twisting it.

To my surprise, after what seemed like forever, I opened my eyes to see him push me forward.

I screamed as I went headlong into the black abyss.

Once my body hit the ground with a thud and a snap, extreme pain seared through my arm. I sat up in the dark, holding my arm, rocking, and waiting for the pain to subside. I knew my arm was broken as I tried to look around.

It was so dark; all I could do was listen as I heard footsteps coming down what seemed to be a ladder. I waited in the darkness for the stranger's next move. I heard a click and light penetrated the darkness, blinding me. When my eyes adjusted, I was shocked by what the bright light uncovered.

I gasped at the sight before me. It wasn't a three or four-foot grave like I imagined. It was more like a fifteen-foot drop to the hard ground.

My eyes widened as I tried to see the face under the brim of the baseball cap. It was still too dark to make him out.

CHAPTER 16

I watched and waited patiently to see what this stranger's next move would be. He seemed to be fiddling with putting the knife up in his pocket and pulling out what looked like a small compass and then opening a folded piece of paper and reading it.

"Get up, you little spoiled witch," he demanded.

My only response was to look at him like he was crazy. In my mind, I figured if this man's intention was to hurt me, he would have done it by now. So I sat and defied his orders.

"Why do you have to make everything so difficult?" the man said as he came over to pull me up.

Sharp fingernails pressed into the back of my shoulders as his grip tightened, pulling me to my feet.

He leaned closer to my face. Chills ran through me as he inhaled my hair.

"Mmm, you smell good enough to eat," he whispered threateningly in my ear.

My breath caught in my throat as I recognized his voice and the phrase he had whispered in my ear before. It was that unusual stranger that had been tailing me everywhere I went.

I pushed at him with my good arm. "It's you! How dare you talk to me like that?"

He laughed. "You never seemed to mind before." He paused, looking down at me. "By the time I'm finished with you, you'll be begging me to kill you."

I could feel anger rise in me like fireworks on the Fourth of July.

"Get away from me, you pervert. You don't scare me," I said, trying to exert confidence, even though every inch of me shook with fear.

A flashback came to me, the way my ex-husband Hank laughed at me because I couldn't find a job in New York. He had made sure I was fired and banned from every agency I went to. Hank had this political pull that tied my hands so every door slammed in my face.

The thought that now this man, like Hank, had the nerve to laugh at me and hold me captive so I couldn't run, had me boiling inside. It was the first time I'd ever felt so mad that if the opportunity presented itself, it would be me slicing his throat. I felt sick and tired of men bullying me to do their will.

"I've had it, you hear me!" I yelled at him and started screaming, hoping Jessie was looking for me by now.

He immediately covered my mouth and pushed me up against the wall.

"You keep your mouth shut and walk," he said as he yanked on my arm and pushed me forward, shining the flashlight down the underground corridor.

"No one will ever hear you in here." He continued to push me forward with his body tight up against my back.

I was confused and disoriented. I knew we were close to my house, but where did this underground corridor lead? Was it another hidden passageway to a hide-out, or possibly a way of escape from the house? And more importantly, how had this moron found it?

The dark, empty corridor seemed to go on forever and every step I took aggravated my arm. My prayer was that Jessie was out of the shower, and not finding me where I was supposed to be, had called Gerald and his posse to come rescue me.

We came to a wooden door that creaked open when he pulled on it. He pushed me through and I felt my face hit a mass of spider webs that sent a chill through me.

"Get in there, you slut, and take a seat," he growled.

I could tell by his voice that he was in a hurry and aggravated at me for making his plan harder than he thought it would be.

The dim light of his flashlight, which seemed to be losing power as he hit it several times, showed an old wooden chair against the wall.

"I said, sit down!" He yelled as I defied him again.

His arm came up with the flashlight and came down with a sizeable force against my neck and shoulder.

He growled at me like an angry dog. "Get your ass in that chair before I end this now."

I wanted to fight him with everything I had, but a still small voice inside said I needed to listen and obey, so all this could be over and done with sooner.

Reluctantly, I sat, and he began using some zip ties from his pocket to anchor my legs to the chair. I held my useless, broken arm close to my chest as it continued to pound with pain. With force, he grabbed my good arm and tied it to the chair. Relief flooded me when he left my other unusable arm alone.

After he knocked a time or two on his flashlight, he shone the light down the corridor to what looked like a wall made of wood.

So great, this is just a freaking hole in the ground that leads nowhere, and the only escape was the way we came in.

"What are you going to do with me?"

I saw white teeth invade the darkness of his face. "You are so naïve. You have no idea what is going on, do you?" He laughed aloud. "I swear you act like a dumb blonde," he said, lifting my long hair from my shoulder and smelling it again.

I was so grossed out by this poor excuse of a man. He had the audacity to touch me. I could feel my stomach knot up and a wave of nausea threaten to spew out.

With a chuckle, he turned and walked towards the door.

"You're not leaving me here, are you?" I asked, trying to keep my voice from trembling.

He never turned around, just continued to chuckle as he left and closed the door behind him, leaving me in the dark. My heart sank when I heard him lock the door from the outside.

CHAPTER 17

I hyperventilated into a full-blown panic attack. The darkness closed up around me, leaving me with no air. I struggled to calm myself, but the air seemed so thin. The blackness suffocated me, making me think I was being buried alive.

As much as I tried to take control I could feel my body shut down to nothingness.

I didn't know how long I was out for, but when I came too I could hear a distant, faint sound from above the ground.

My lungs expanded as I yelled and yelled, "I'm here, I'm here, I'm here!"

I stopped and listened as the sounds seemed to be moving away.

"No! Please don't leave me," I cried.

I screamed and screamed, but to no avail. No one came. No one heard me.

Why couldn't they find the hidden escape hatch on the ground above? Were they idiots? I'm here, I'm here, I yelled again.

In the darkness, I waited for some sign of life above ground, but nothing happened. No one came back. My heart sank. I was so sure Jessie would find me. He just had to.

After what seemed like hours of pulling and twisting in the chair, exhaustion took over and my head fell forward as I slipped into unconsciousness.

"Sarah... Sarah," I heard a faint voice in the corner of the room.

Lifting my head weakly, I focused on a small penlight that appeared by the far wall. The light became bigger and bigger. As I watched, a figure appear. It looked like my Aunt Pauline with her long white hair.

A light scent of Chantilly perfume drifted up to my nose. My eyes widened. Oh, my God! It wasn't Aunt Pauline. It was my mom. My mom wore Chantilly perfume and looked so much like Aunt Pauline. They both had long white hair that they put up in buns on their head. The Chantilly perfume gave it away.

"Mom? Mom? What are you doing here?" I asked.

She pointed to the wall. Was she showing me the way out? I wondered. Again, the spirits of this world were coming to my aid. My mind went back to one of the most difficult times of my life when I was days from being evicted from my apartment in New York and an angel showed me the way.

I mumbled, "Thank you, thank you, thank you."

The sound of my voice saying thank you roused me. I was disappointed to find myself still in the dark, tied to a chair and not in my soft, cozy bed with Jessie.

I felt this stab in my heart as I realized it was only a dream. My eyes watered, spilling tears down my face as my heart ached. I didn't want to die down here like Aunt Pauline. They left her in the cellar to die in a chair. Oh my God, I couldn't let this happen. I had to fight.

"I have to fight. I will fight," I said aloud as if I was coaching myself.

I wiggled and pulled and pulled. I tried to jump, moving the old wooden chair inches from its spot.

I put every ounce of energy into the next jump. Once the chair hit the ground with as much force as I could exert, I heard it crack. I knew I was making headway. I jumped up one more time and when I hit the ground; the chair broke, spilling me onto the damp, cool earth.

I pushed and banged on the door, hoping the dampness in the tunnel had been enough to cause rot in the wood as it had in the chair.

With no success, I cautiously made my way against the wall to the other end of the corridor. Again, I pushed and kicked and banged against the wall.

Then it came to me, the dream I had. My mom was pointing to the wall close to the corner. My mom and I were almost alike in every way. We were even the same height. So I positioned myself the way I saw her in my dream. I put my arm out the way she did, then I touched the wall around the same spot.

I gasped in excitement as my hand passed over what seemed to be a nail protruding from the wood.

I pulled on the nail and then pushed on the nail, but nothing happened. Then I tried to move it side to side, and it slipped easily to the left. Hearing a click, I knew I had found the answer to the puzzle.

After hearing the click, I pulled on the nail and the wall gave way to a passageway. It was still so dark, and I didn't know where I was and what to expect.

I slid my foot forward inch by inch, hoping there wasn't a drop off into another tunnel lower than the dirt floor I was on.

My hand extended in the darkness, trying to find a wall to follow. Relief flooded my soul when my hand hit what felt like another wooden wall. Cautiously, I moved forward. I came across what felt like a shelf. Moving my hand across the shelf slowly and deliberately, I hit something. I examined the objects until I realized it was some glass jars.

That's when it hit me. I was in the basement of my house.

CHAPTER 18

I knew from memory that the ladder was just on the other side of the shelf. With careful steps, my hand hit the ladder, and I grabbed it with all my might. Tears flowed from my eyes with gratitude.

In the dark, I whispered, "Thank you, mom. Thank you for always being there for me."

I looked up the ladder, hoping for some kind of light. Oh well, I thought. I can do this. One step at a time, I ascended the ladder until I hit the floor of the closet with my head. Pushing through the slats of the floor, I felt them give way as shoes and other items from the closet floor fell past me onto the basement floor.

With excitement thrumming through my body, I climbed out and felt for the handle of the closet door.

I was out. I was safe. But... but the house was quiet and empty. I found the hallway switch and turned it on.

My mouth dropped as I heard my own gasp from my lips. Someone trashed the place. There were drawers open on the small table by the door and papers on the floor. When I looked into the living room, the coffee table had been moved and the books from the bookshelf were all on the ground.

Moving the curtain aside, I found my car still parked outside. Why was it so quiet? Where was Jessie?

Dying of thirst, I walked to the kitchen and turned on the light. The drawers and kitchen cabinets were all open, as though someone had been searching for something. Is that what that slob wanted, to ransack my house? So he left me in that hole in the ground and trashed my house? Surely he wasn't a treasure seeker, too. If I hadn't been so weak, I would have laughed at that ridiculous idea. I smiled at that thought, and with my good arm, I grabbed a glass from the drain-board and filled it with icy water from the refrigerator. It felt like a rainstorm in a desert going down my throat as the cool water took away the dry, parched feel in my mouth and throat.

How long had I been gone? Where was everyone? Something felt off.

With my legs feeling like noodles, I carefully made my way to my bedroom with dread in my heart and a brick in my stomach. What if that man was still in my house? I turned on the light and the bed was empty. As I looked down towards the floor, my eyes caught sight of blood leading to the hidden passageway in the wall by the bed. I gasped.

Oh Lord, please tell me all of this has been a dream. Jessie, please wake me up, I begged. Don't let this dread in my heart continue.

I was reliving my dream, only I wasn't covered in blood. In my weakened state, I tried to move. My legs were heavy weights as I drug myself to the side table and found my small flashlight. My hand went to my chest as I struggled to breathe. There was no air. Sarah, you can't pass out now, you have to see this through; I told myself. My hands shook with the reality that I might find the worst thing imaginable on the other side of the hidden panel. Giving the panel one good push, it clicked open. With my heart beating out my chest and my body shaking, I pulled to open the hidden doorway. The passageway was clear except for the trail of blood all the way to the ladder at the far wall. With heaviness in my heart, I climbed the stairs to the next floor.

I stood there in the dark, trying to turn on the flashlight. My hand shook so badly I fumbled around until I found the button.

The bright light exposed the opened cubicles on the left wall and the empty table in the corner.

"Uh," a weak voice penetrated the dark, still night. It came from the floor.

I slowly shined the light down to find Jessie lying there in a pool of blood. My deepest dread from my nightmare had come to pass. They hurt my Jessie.

I dropped to my knees beside him in the warm, thick blood. As I leaned closer, I reached out my shaking hand and the worst feeling in the world tried to consume me.

"Sarah... you're... okay?" he whispered in a voice so weak it was almost inaudible.

"Yes, I'm here sweetheart. I'm here."

"Sarah," he struggled to say as his hand came up to touch my face. "I love you."

"Oh my God, Jessie. Please hold on. Please don't leave me. I love you, too."

Tears ran down my face as I watched the man I love, take his last breath.

"No! No! No!" I screamed, laying my head on his chest as my body convulsed with weeping. "Jessie, please don't go. Please don't leave me here alone. Please, Jessie, please," I wailed into his chest.

"I need to get help. Please don't leave me, Jessie. I'll get help." I moved forward and kissed him on the lips. I grabbed my flashlight and stood up. The room swayed as I lost my balance and tilted backward. When my body hit the wall, I felt thankful I didn't fall to the floor. I wasn't sure I would have made it up again. My body was weak and my head was fuzzy. Unconsciousness threatened to end me there where I stood.

Sarah, don't give up now. You have to call Gerald; I told myself.

I forced myself to move forward, opening the wall to the second floor. Deliberately moving my body, I exited the hidden room. Trying to hold myself up, I grabbed the banister and struggled to descend the staircase to the first floor. The weight of my body was like moving hundreds of pounds of cement as I moved in slow motion. I was struggling to pick up my phone as the room swayed. I pressed the number one on speed dial to call Gerald.

I could hear Gerald on the other end of the phone, but I couldn't talk. Thank God he had caller ID.

"Sarah, is that you?" As hard as I tried to respond, all I could say was "Yes."

"I'm coming, Sarah," he said with urgency.
The room spun, and I fell to the floor, out cold.

CHAPTER 19

The powerful smell of alcohol invaded my nostrils and a warm, gentle hand massaging my skin roused me from the unknown. Trying to open my eyes, I asked, "Jessie?"

"Sarah, it's Gerald." I heard in reply as I finally came to.

My gaze settled on Gerald's face. I had never seen his face so distressed before.

I looked around and didn't recognize my surroundings. "Where am I?"

"You're at the hospital. You had a pretty nasty bump on your head and you broke your arm."

It hit me like a ton of bricks. The hit on the head, being thrown down a hole and breaking my arm and being tied down in the dark. "Jessie!" I yelled, trying to sit up.

Gerald gently laid me back down. "Jessie…"

"Oh, Gerald, no," I said, searching his face. "Please tell me it's not so." Tears formed in my eyes. The worried, drawn look on his face said it all. I couldn't help it, my heart was broken, and the weeping came in tidal waves.

Gerald gently pulled me up in his arms, holding me tight as I let Niagara Falls flow down my face.

My chest ached as if it was broken in two. My life was over. I lost the one true thing that made me feel protected, alive, and loved.

As my sobbing lessened, Gerald loosened his grip and handed me a Kleenex. "I know it's hard, Sarah, but you have to be strong right now. You have been through a lot and we need to catch the criminal that did this. Can you help me with that?" Gerald tilted my head up. "Sarah, can you help me?"

Sniffing and wiping my eyes, I realized I wasn't getting anywhere with all my blubbering. I sat up straight while uncontrollable tears automatically ran down my face. "Gerald, I will do everything in my power to help you catch this guy. Just name it. What do you need?"

He reached in his pocket to pull out a small notebook. "What did he look like?"

Tears continued to flow as I tried to relive that awful night. My mind went blank. "Oh, Gerald, I don't know."

"Didn't you see him? Is he the same man that you have had encounters with?"

"Yes! That's him. He's a little taller than me. His belly protrudes way over his belt," I said, motioning my one good arm out from my body.

"You said he had light-colored hair, right?" Gerald asked, cocking his head to look at me from his notebook.

"Yes, sort of dirty blond or sandy colored. Oh, Gerald, I'm not sure. But I remember he had a light complexion."

"What color eyes?"

Every time I'd had contact with this person, I deliberately moved my face away from his, not wanting to look at him. Not wanting him to touch me. What color eyes did he have? "Gerald, I'm not sure… but I think they were dark."

"I think you're right. Remember how I found someone at the end of your driveway? This fits the description perfectly. What did he say to you? Did he divulge his plans to you?"

I hung my head down and whispered, "No, he said nothing."

"Is there anything else you can say about all this?" Gerald asked.

"I'm so sorry, Gerald. I wish I could help you more. The only thing is… I feel he is another treasure hunter."

"That's okay. I think I have enough information." He patted my arm. "I'll be back bright and early in the morning to bring you home. So get some rest and I'll see you then."

"Gerald, before you go," I said, grabbing his arm. "Where is Jessie?"

I watched as he rubbed his face, leaving a red hue. "He's in the morgue, here at the hospital."

"I was too late. I couldn't save him," I mumbled with my head down, tears running down my face again.

Gerald sat on the edge of my bed. "If I hadn't left to get more help, this wouldn't have happened." I watched his face as a tear formed in the corner of his eye. "I never should have left."

I felt so bad. I pulled myself up with my good arm and hugged him tightly.

We both were feeling guilty for not saving Jessie, a memory that would haunt our souls for the rest of our lives.

"This just makes me more determined than ever to find that maniac. He will pay for his crime even if I have to..."

"Don't say it, Gerald. I know you loved Jessie as much as I did, but please don't do something unlawful and lose your job."

Gerald cleared his throat and stood up. "I'll try, but I will not swear by it. But hear what I say, Sarah Hamilton. I swear we will catch this man and he will get what's coming to him. Nobody messes with mine and gets away with it."

Gerald sauntered to the door, then turned, "You're lucky to be alive, Sarah. If only I hadn't gone back to the office, I would have been there. I'm sorry..." Gerald stood straight, then said, "But everything will be all right. You'll see."

As I watched the door close, I couldn't help but feel bad for him. After he left to go back to the station, I knew we both had lost a part of our lives that we could never get back. How could we manage to go on without the powerful strength of Jessie?

Then it hit me. Jessie's parents hadn't watched that last sunset with us; they'd turned around to look at Jessie. Had they known this would happen? Couldn't they have intervened like my mom did in the dream, showing me the way out of that dark, damp place? Couldn't they have warned us?

A nurse came in, taking my mind off my thoughts, and added a syringe of something into my drip and in a matter of seconds I was out.

Sometime in the night, I felt someone on my bed. I groggily looked up to see that awful slob of a man leaning in close to my face.

"So, you made it out. You won't be so lucky next time."

I swung my good arm trying to hit him and missed. I bolted to a sitting position to find no one. Oh my God, was I dreaming? But it had looked so real. I lay back down, but the odor of stale beer and sweat lingered. There was no way I was dreaming. He was here at the hospital. That was the last thing I remembered.

CHAPTER 20

True to his word, Gerald was there just as I was being released. There was a terrible quietness between us as he pushed me to his car in a wheelchair.

With my seatbelt buckled, I turned to look at him. His eyes were swollen, and he had stubble forming on his face. I noticed he was wearing the same uniform from yesterday with the mustard stain on his collar. He must have been up all night.

"Do you want me to stop anywhere before we get to your house?"

"No," I replied, realizing I didn't want to go home. There was nothing for me there, just a cold, empty house with no life and only troubles. The troubles I would have to face alone now. Jessie said he would never leave me. But he did. He left me when I needed him most.

We pulled up at the house, and Gerald, being the gentleman he was, came and opened the door for me. I stood looking up at the house that had given me so much misery since the day I'd arrived.

Dragging my feet, I stumbled and almost fell. Gerald reached out to grab me. "Be careful, Sarah."

"What does it matter now? Jessie is gone, never to return. My life is over," I managed to say in my weakened state.

"Sarah, please don't think like that. We will get that son-of-a-bitch and he will be locked up forever."

"You may get him, but it won't bring Jessie back," I said as tears fell again.

Gerald helped me up the stairs and into the house and into my favorite recliner, Old Blue.

I patted my recliner with my good arm. "Old blue, still here to comfort me in my hard times."

"You named your recliner?" Gerald asked as he sat on the couch.

"The only thing I can depend on. This recliner has been with me longer than my marriage to Hank. Good times and bad, Old Blue is always here."

I noticed the look on Gerald's face. He thinks I'm crazy.

"What kind of medicine does the doctor have you on, anyway?"

I handed him my pill bottle for pain and Gerald nodded. "Okay, do you need some water or something before I go?"

"Yes, please. I have some bottled water in the fridge if you don't mind."

"I don't mind at all. By the way, I cleaned up the mess the best I could." He paused, looking strange. "Please don't go into the secret passageway or in the basement until I get the FBI out here."

"The FBI? Why do they need to come out here again?"

"They insisted on being informed about anything else going on in this house."

"I don't understand," I said, shaking my head, trying to clear away the pressure between my eyes that was trying to take control of my thoughts.

"They still consider the death of your Aunt as unsolved, and they want answers as much as I do."

"So, you have been keeping them informed of everything?"

"Yes, it's my duty to work with them until we iron everything out."

"They want all the answers, but they give us none. Was that even my Aunt's body in the basement? Why weren't they here to keep that filthy, dirty man from kidnapping me or saving Jessie? And why can't they do something about that crooked lawyer, Brian Thibodeaux? I'm sorry to say, but I just don't trust anybody anymore." I paused, watching Gerald's face fall. "Except you and Jessie, I mean," I uttered softly, hoping not to hurt his feelings after all he had done for me and Jessie.

"I understand," he replied, patting my hand. "I'll get that water."

With my water in hand, I contemplated if I should tell Gerald of the close encounter I had last night. "Gerald I… I'm not sure if it was a dream, or real. But he was there in my room last night."

95

"He what!" he yelled. "Are you telling me that kidnapping son-of-a-bitch was in your room?"

"I'm not sure; it could have been a dream. I was heavily sedated. But it seemed real, and I can still remember that awful smell. He has a terrible body odor. A mixture of beer, sweat, and just nastiness."

Gerald took the cap from his head and slapped his thigh with it in anger. "Again, I leave and you're in danger."

I watched as he paced back and forth between me and the front door. "I don't know what to say. I'm sorry I wasn't there."

"Gerald, please don't beat yourself up over this. This man obviously doesn't want to kill me, or he would have. For some reason, he wants me alive."

"Well, I guess you're right about that." Gerald sat on the coffee table and reached to take my hand. "I promise you, I will find out what's going on. I won't let anything happen to you. Just give me some time."

"You sound like Jessie," I whispered sadly, my head down, trying to stop the need to cry again.

"We have a plan, Sarah. Just get some rest and I'll be back to check on you."

"We?" I asked, confused by his statement.

"The department and myself. We will get to the bottom of this."

I sat there listening to Gerald's car fade away on the gravel driveway, as an immense feeling of emptiness settled in my heart.

The house seemed so quiet and hollow. "Oh Jessie, why did you leave me?" I whispered under my breath.

I wiped the tears from my face. "You said you would never leave me."

I sat on Old Blue and pulled my legs up and hugged them. My head fell to my knees, and I cried, knowing my life would never be the same again.

CHAPTER 21

I gripped the arm of the wooden rocking chair on the front porch as a seed of loneliness continued to manifest in thoughts of bleak despair. Today, it wasn't even worth the effort to dress, comb my hair, or put on make-up.

The nightmare of the previous days dulled the beauty of the swamps, and my heart ached with shooting pains of loss unimaginable to express. Losing Jessie was the hardest thing that had ever happened to me. I didn't care that I was kidnapped and held prisoner deep underground by a psychotic maniac or thrown into a hole so deep that I broke my arm. None of that mattered, nothing mattered.

Gerald, our trusted friend and Sheriff pulled up, climbed the stairs, and stood before me while I was mentally in a land of darkness. Not sure when I noticed his steady presence standing beside me, but it didn't seem to matter that he just stood there motionless, staring at me.

"Gerald, when did you get here?" I struggled to say.

"Cher, you're not looking too good. Did you get any sleep last night?"

"Sleep?" For the life of me, I couldn't remember if I slept or not. I couldn't bear that big empty bed without Jessie's warm body next to me and listening to his calm rhythmic breathing that always soothed my soul. Without my bed, all I remember is trying to stretch out on the couch. Then, after tossing and turning, I made my way to Old Blue and somehow ended up on the porch.

"Stay here, I'll be right back," Gerald said as he walked into the house.

I wasn't going anywhere. What was the point, my life was over? How could I go on without Jessie? The emptiness was more than I could stand.

Minutes or hours later, who knows, Gerald walked back out on the porch. "Here, drink this," Gerald insisted, handing me a cup of hot coffee.

I sat there with the cup in my hands, staring off into space. The warm morning sun shone through the trees. The fall colors blasting, an array of bright colors around me seemed dull compared to the memory of the fall colors in New York. All I could do was sit wrapped up in a blanket while my heart told my brain this is the end of my life.

"Sarah, you need to snap out of it. I need you to pull yourself together. We have work to do."

"I don't see how I can help you today, Gerald," I said weakly, not caring what he had on his mind.

"If Jessie was here, he would be so upset with you."

That got my attention. I looked up. "Upset with me? What did I do?"

"It's not what you did, it's what you're not doing that would upset him. You know, Jessie. He would be retracing his steps, digging into what happened, and why. He wouldn't give up until he knew who the perpetrator was, and he wouldn't stop until he had him in cuffs and on his way to jail."

A tear ran down my cheek. He was right. Jessie would investigate, pursue, and hunt down that dangerous criminal and make sure all loose ends were tied up. He wouldn't rest until the job was done.

"I know you're right, but… I can't make my heart move forward. Maybe in a couple of months, I'll be able to think about this better."

Gerald reached over and touched my arm. "I'm sorry for your loss, Sarah, but Jessie was my friend, too, and because we were friends, I want that S.O.B. to be locked up for the rest of his life. Don't you want that, too?"

That's when I noticed Gerald's face. He looked like he had been through a war. He had dark circles under his eyes with a five o'clock shadow growing on his face. His eyes were bloodshot and his face looked hollow. The worst part was the deep, dark look of despair all over his face.

I nodded my head. "Yes, more than anything."

Gerald lifted my hand that was still gripping the warm cup and raised it to my mouth. "Drink your coffee and let's get down to business."

I sipped the warm fluid that I once thought had the most wonderful flavor but now went down like dull, tasteless sludge. It was funny; when all was right with the world and you had love in your heart, the world seemed so alive. The colors were more vibrant, the smells more aromatic; the foods had a flavor that exploded in your mouth and best of all touch was more intense than anything else in the world. But when there was a deep loss in your life, everything became dark and dull in comparison. It was like living in one of those old black-and-white TV shows. No color, no taste, no smells, and worst of all, no touch.

I needed to motivate myself, pull myself up from the grave, and move forward.

Gerald pulled a chair beside me and blew on the steaming liquid.

Every normalcy of life was now strange and uneasy. The routine of Jessie waking me each morning to the rich aroma of dark-ground coffee was replaced by the parish Sheriff making me coffee. If the deep despair would let some light shine in, I would have thought this very amusing. If Jessie was here, he would laugh at this scenario.

Gerald cleared his throat, gulped the last drop of coffee, and said, "Okay, you already gave me a description of the perpetrator. What I need to know is, are you sure he didn't say anything about what his plans were?"

"No, not that I remember."

"Start from the beginning. Jessie told me he went to take a shower while you cleaned up the kitchen after an excellent gumbo."

"Jessie said my gumbo was excellent?"

Gerald smiled for the first time. "Yeah, he said, he finally got that city girl to cook one of the best gumbos around."

The corner of my mouth lifted a little. A small, thin ray of light hit my heart with joy. He loved my gumbo. "I had never really learned to cook until I got here."

"I know." Gerald cleared his throat again. "Jessie said you went out to throw the scraps in the bayou and you didn't come to tell him you were back. He said when you didn't return he cut his shower short and walked out looking for you."

"Someone hit me. I didn't see him on the porch. He came out of nowhere." I paused.

"Go on."

"I remember coming to as he was pulling me off the porch. I did try to get away. I knew how important it is to get away as soon as possible." I hung my head down. "But it didn't work. He was strong."

I sat for a minute in thought. "What I don't understand is… how did he know about the hole in the ground?"

"Can you show me where this hole is?"

"Yeah, I think so." I got up to walk to the backyard and realized I wasn't dressed yet and had no shoes on my feet. "Let me slip some shoes on. Meet me on the back porch."

After a couple of minutes dressing in yesterday's clothes and slipping on some shoes, we stood on the back porch while I described the hit and where he drug my body down the stairs.

"I tried to scream. He smothered my mouth with thick, black gloves. Leather, I think. I ran towards the front, but he grabbed me. I fell, I think. I don't remember." My head was hurting so much that I used my hand to put pressure on my temple.

"Did he carry you off?"

"No, yes, I think he pushed and carried me that way," I said, extending my arm towards the boundary of the yard.

"Show me," Gerald insisted.

We walked until the yard ended, and the woods began. I turned around to look at the house. No, we had walked further in.

After we walked several yards more, I said, "It was here. I think." I held my jaw, wondering where the trapdoor was.

Gerald started kicking some limbs and leaves around.

I looked back at the house again. It was the wrong angle. "No, wait. There. Try there." I pointed about two feet ahead of me.

I looked around again. "It's here, I'm sure of it."

Gerald again was on the ground swiping leaves around until the corner of the trap door showed. He hurriedly pushed some more leaves away and lifted the lid from the hole.

He reached behind him for a small flashlight attached to his belt.

"Look here." I pointed. "There's a ladder."

He shone the light deep in the hole for an unrestricted view. "I'll go first."

I stepped back. "I... I don't think I can go down there again."

Gerald searched my face for a minute and put his hand on my shoulder. "It's okay. I'll go investigate this myself."

I could feel a chill start at my feet and work its way up as I watched Gerald descend the ladder and disappear into the hole.

Holding my sweater closed, I looked around to see if anyone was watching us. I tried to hold myself together as my head swayed. Making small steps backward, I leaned up against a tree to keep from falling. I didn't want to relive this nightmare again.

My body felt so weak that I slid down against the tree to a sitting position and waited.

It didn't feel like Gerald would ever come back. I waited and waited. My nerves were shot, and I didn't know how much more of all this I could take.

CHAPTER 22

Reluctantly, I crawled over to the hole. "Gerald?" I yelled.

There was no sound. Carefully, I decided to descend into the depth of the black abyss.

"Gerald?" I called out again once my feet hit solid ground. I turned on the flashlight on my phone.

With small, cautious steps, I made my way down the gloomy tunnel to the wooden door. It was quiet and cold. Swallowing hard, I entered the chamber where I broke the chair I was tied to.

"Gerald?"

"I'm here," he announced from the ground where he examined the chair. "You're lucky this chair was rotten. If not, you may have been down here a long time."

"Don't remind me." I felt the deep despair of that night. "I… I yelled, but no one heard me." Slowly, I turned to look around.

"He left me here, alone, in the dark. He left out the same door."

Gerald stood. "What did you do next?"

"I'm not sure. I don't know if I passed out or what, but…"

"But what?" Gerald asked, eager to know more.

"I had a vision. It was my mom. She was standing there." I walked to the opposite side of the room and showed Gerald where she was and what she did. "She showed me the way out."

Gerald didn't look at me like I was crazy. He encouraged me to go on.

"This is another door," I said, pushing through to the basement.

We both cautiously walked into the dark, dank basement. Gerald took his cap off and scratched his head.

"I never would have believed it. We searched this basement with a fine-tooth comb and never saw this door."

"Why would you? When you close the door, it looks just like the basement wall. Even the FBI didn't see it."

"You mean Tweedledee and Tweedledum?" Gerald chuckled. "Jessie told me all about it."

I laughed, remembering two well-dressed FBI agents coming out the basement covered in mud from head to toe, still in their expensive suit and tie. Jessie and I both laughed about that for days.

It felt good to laugh, but remembering Jessie's contagious laughter hit my heart like a hammer.

"What did you do then?"

"After I realized where I was, I climbed the ladder to the closet and got out."

Gerald searched my face. "Is that when you found Jessie?"

"The house was ransacked as I searched for him. When I got to the bedroom, that's when my nightmare hit me."

"Are you talking about a literal nightmare?"

"I dreamed this... all this blood was going into the secret panel, but Jessie always woke me before I found out where the blood went or what was causing it." I paused with my head hanging. "But he wasn't here to stop me this time."

Tears flowed again. Gerald's hand reached out to console me. "Come on; let's get out of this basement."

I inhaled deeply the cool, fresh air on the front porch thankful this was over.

Gerald stood before me and said, "I need you to come out of this depression and take some action. Lock up everything as soon as you can. I believe this is not over yet. Do you understand? Jessie would never forgive me if something happened to you. I want to know everyone you see and everyone you talk to. If you ever feel like, there is something wrong I want to know ASAP. Any time of day or night you call me. Do you understand?"

"Yes, Gerald... I understand."

"Now before I go, let's go look and see if the camera caught anything?"

"Oh, my God! I never thought of that." We immediately went to the computer to research the last several days.

After watching intently, trying to get a good handle on that dramatic night, my mouth dropped as I watched how some of the town came together. My sweet love and Gerald were running ragged looking for me. They would pass so close to the trap door, never giving it a second thought that I could be in a hole in the ground right under their feet.

Viewing the scenes unfold before us, we came to the point where most of the people had left for the night and Jessie and Gerald were the only ones left.

"Here's where I went back to the station to try to round up some fresh eyes to look some more. We wanted to expand outside the property lines and deep in the woods. I needed more eyes."

In my mind, I figured this was probably about the time my mom showed up to show me the way out.

"There he is," Gerald said.

"It's not very clear, but I know that's him." I paused. "If only I had gotten loose sooner, I might have been able to save Jessie."

Gerald's hand went around my shoulder. "Don't talk like that, Sarah. You can't change what has happened, and it's not your fault." Gerald's head hung down.

"I promise you I'll get that son-of-a-bitch if it is the last thing I do."

"Gerald, you're a good friend so don't take this wrong, but... don't promise me something you can't fulfill."

"What I say, I mean. As long as I'm Sheriff I'll never stop searching for this guy."

"Yeah, well, Jessie promised he would never leave me and where is he now?"

"He's not gone, Sarah."

"What?" I looked around. "Do you see him here now? Don't go talking shit to me, Gerald. I'm not in the mood for it," I yelled and stormed out the room.

I scrambled to the bathroom to cry. I looked in the mirror. "What is wrong with you, Sarah? Gerald has always been here for you. You are not being fair to him." I blew my nose, washed my face, and walked back out to Gerald like a dog with his tail between his legs and his ears down.

"I'm sorry, Gerald. I didn't mean it," I said as another tear ran down my face.

"It's okay, Cher; I understand what you are going through. I mean what I say," he said, tapping the brim of his cap and giving me a wink. "Now come help me move some of your furniture in front of the closet door. We don't want anyone coming in through the basement, do we?"

I went to the closet door and looked around the floor to make sure the lid to the basement was still in place. Something seemed off. Something was missing.

"Gerald, did you see that god awful dress of Aunt Pauline's when you picked up everything? You know the one with all the gaudy jewels on it."

"No, why, is it missing?"

I slid one piece of clothes after another. "It's gone. You don't think someone actually thought that dress had real jewels sewn on it, do you?"

He pushed his cap up and scratched his head. "Well, it crossed my mind. If the rumor is true about the hidden money and jewels from a heist in France, then it could have been a possibility."

"I didn't notice him leave the house with the dress or anything else."

"I didn't see that either. So, if it was real, he probably won't be back. But if that dress was a fake, he won't give up looking until he finds what he is looking for."

He pulled his cap back down and winked at me. "Okay, let's move this in front of the door. All you need to do is just push. Push with your hip and don't hurt your arm. I will pick up extra locks and latches for you. I have to get back to work, but I will be back later this afternoon."

CHAPTER 23

Several hours later, I heard a knock on the door. I opened the door, hoping for Gerald, but was slapped in the face with shock as Brian Thibodeaux stood before me.

"What the hell do you want?" I demanded.

"Listen, I know you're mad at me, but I wanted to remind you that there is someone who wants to buy your place. I figure since you've gone through so much lately that you may want to consider this offer and then you can go back to New York and start over."

"I haven't forgotten. Is there anything else you want?" I asked, holding my ground at the door.

"No, you have my number," he said, and he walked away.

I stood at the door just to make sure he'd really left. There had been so much going on that I really didn't remember he knew someone who wanted this house, if that was even true. Considering this lawyer has lied to me more than once.

A small, warm glow lit up in my heart as I thought about leaving and starting over again in my hometown, New York. Things would never be the same here without Jessie. I wasn't sure I was strong enough to keep on going, looking over my shoulder and not sleeping at night in this house of mystery. I wasn't sure I wanted to be here anymore.

I felt more alive after Brian's visit. In my mind, I was already making plans to leave.

The sun had set, and I made a walk-through in the house, checking every window and door. I stood at the bottom of the stairs debating on checking upstairs when I saw something move.

My hand went to my chest, and I stepped back. From out of nowhere, that old wheelchair from up in the attic stood at the top of the stairs.

I took one more step back and someone knocked on the door, making me jump out my skin.

I turned to open the door and saw Gerald. My body automatically deflated with a long sigh. I looked back at the stairs and there was nothing there.

This made little sense. Was I seeing things? Was it the pain medicine?

"Gerald, come in. I was just debating on a trip upstairs to make sure everything was in order and locked up when you got here." I paused, looking back at the top of the stairs. "Would you come with me?"

"Let's go," Gerald said, placing a bag on the side table and turning on the light switch at the bottom of the stairs.

Gerald walked up about three steps while my feet were glued to the floor. "Are you coming?"

"I, I..."

"It's okay, Sarah. I can go check everything out. You stay here."

A sigh of relief hit me, causing my shoulders to relax as I listened to Gerald's footsteps walk back and forth.

When Gerald walked to the top of the stairs he smiled. "Everything is in order."

"Thank God," I replied. "Come sit in the living room, I need to tell you about a visit I had today."

I watched Gerald descend the stairs with one eyebrow cocked up.

We both sat on the couch. "Please don't give me awful news, Sarah. It's been a long hard day."

I couldn't speak. What I had to say was awful news.

"Well?" Gerald asked.

"Well, you said not to say anything bad." I paused.

"Well, you can't leave me hanging here. What happened today?"

"Brian Thibodeaux came by today."

"What? Is he starting shit again?" Gerald asked angrily.

"Well... no. He reminded me that someone wants to buy the house."

"You're not considering this, are you?"

"Well, yeah. I can go back home."

"What about Jessie?" He asked, leaning forward like he was ready to jump from the couch.

"I don't have Jessie anymore. Without him, my life here is over. I need a fresh start. I hate being reminded in every room in this house about Jessie. I can't bear it." A strong stab penetrated my heart, causing tears to flow down my cheek.

Gerald's head hung down. He looked a million miles away.

His face rose slowly with moistened eyes. Was he about to cry? I wondered.

"I need your help, Sarah. Please don't make any hasty decisions. I know it's hard, but we need to catch this guy. Give me a few months and if you still feel this way, I'll pack you myself."

I hated to see the look on Gerald's face. "Gerald, I'm scared. If that man had the tenacity to walk up in here and shoot Jessie for money, there's no telling what he will do to me when he comes back."

"I'll do everything in my power to keep you safe. You will not be alone. Since I have to be on the job a lot, I'll have people passing by your house several times a day, and... I'll come by every day if you let me."

I giggled. "When have I ever stopped you from coming by? Mi casa, es tu casa." He was trying so hard to keep me here and safe that I couldn't help but agree. I nodded.

"Okay, I'll stay and see how things turn out. Now, how about some of my famous leftover gumbo before you leave?"

"I'd be honored," he said with a slight nod.

CHAPTER 24

I finally slept the night through, even though it was on the couch. It hurt way too much to sleep in our bed, and the bed felt two miles wide with no one else in it.

In my heart, I knew I needed to get a routine going in my life if I was going to try to stay, at least a little while longer.

Gerald had left an array of locks, latches, and deadbolts on the side table. The first thing on my agenda was to find some tools.

That's when I remembered Jessie had a box of tools on the side of the house by the fireplace.

I walked out on the porch as my eyes watered from the brightness. The sun may have been bright, but it sure was cold. The cold in Louisiana was a moist cold that went through your clothes to your bones. I pulled Aunt Pauline's jacket collar up to my chin and made my way to the side of the house. That's when it hit me. I remembered something shiny in the bricks of the fireplace when I tried to escape from my intruder.

With my curiosity taking over, I reached into the hole where the brick had fallen from and found something shiny and silver. I turned it over in my hand examining it and realized it was some kind of key. It wasn't flat like most keys. It had a circular bottom to it. How strange, I thought.

"Hello, excuse me," I heard from the front side of the house causing my breath to catch in my throat.

A tall young man started walking towards me as I slowly put the key in my pocket.

There was something familiar about this guy, but I couldn't put my finger on it.

He watched me put the key in my pocket and smiled. "I didn't mean to scare you, but I need to talk to you."

He kept walking towards me, which gave me an uneasy feeling. "Stop right there," I demanded.

Looking behind me, I wondered if I should run to the back door but realized it was locked. The only way back in the house was through the front door.

"What do you want?" I asked, feeling trapped.

"I'm not sure if you remember me, but I'm Billy Joe."

"Billy Joe, the guy that broke into my house?"

"Yes, ma'am. That's why I'm here."

I started walking towards him, but made a big circle around him, trying to avoid him reaching out and grabbing me. My mind was grasping at ways to get away from this young man as soon as possible.

Once I reached the front porch, I noticed that Billy Joe was following me. "I said stay right there, where I can see you."

When I had my hand on the door handle of the house I turned and asked, "So what is it you want?"

He started to walk closer.

"No!" I yelled, putting the palm of my hand out to him.

He looked down at the ground, then looked up. "I don't blame you for being scared of me; after all, I was in your house and moving your bed while you slept."

"Was it you or Hank moving my bed every night?"

"Well, we both did."

"How the hell did you get mixed up with Hank, anyway?" I had to know.

"It was through a mutual friend. But that's not why I'm here."

"Okay then, why are you here?"

"My mom told me I need to apologize to you for breaking into your house," he said with his head down like a scolded puppy.

"Your mom wants you to apologize? So does that mean you don't want to apologize?"

"No, ma'am, I mean it, too. She made me realize that if the tables were turned and someone broke in on my mom, how mad I'd be. So I need to ask for your forgiveness and offer my services. You know if you need help around here or anything." He paused. "No charge."

"No charge, huh?" I smiled.

"Well, I kind of owe you and we heard the dreadful news about your handyman."

"My handyman?" It felt bad that they saw the love of my life as just a handyman around here.

"Yeah, he did an outstanding job on your house." He looked up at the house with a sparkle of admiration.

"Well, Billy Joe, I'll have to think about this."

"Here is my phone number." He dug in his jacket pocket and pulled out a card and placed it on the edge of the porch.

"I'm legit now, see. I have my own business cards and all. Mom said she was tired of my loafing around and wanted me to do something with my life. So, I figure if I'm handy at breaking into places, then I'd be handy at fixing places," he announced with his head tilted and a slight upward movement of the corner of his mouth.

I couldn't help but be amused by his actions. "As I said, I'll think about it."

"Okay then."

I watched him walk down to the edge of my property and get in a small white truck with someone in it. My eyes strained to see his passenger, but couldn't make anything out.

After working all afternoon putting on locks and latches, I was ready for something cold to drink. I poured a glass of ice tea and relaxed on Old Blue, eager to talk to Gerald about my visit today.

I couldn't help but wonder why now that Billy Joe came around. Was it true he was sorry and just wanted to help? Or had Hank hired him to get close to me so he could continue to look for the hidden treasure?

It's a shame that there were only two people I trusted in this world: Jessie and Gerald.

"And now we're down to one."

CHAPTER 25

Footsteps on the porch and a knock on the door roused me to the world of reality.

I started to unlock and open the door as usual, but fear gripped my chest so tight I decided to look out the window first.

With a sigh of relief, I was excited to see Gerald.

"Come in, Gerald. Boy, do I have news for you today."

"Me too," Gerald replied.

"You first," I insisted.

"I got word today that the FBI won't be coming. They said since it wasn't a member of their organization that died, that it's our problem. So don't be waiting up for any help from them," Gerald growled.

"Oh, I see. I thought they wanted to be informed on everything going on here?"

"Well, that's it. They want to be informed but don't want to help. So, what's your news?" he asked as he went to the kitchen to pour himself some coffee.

I followed behind him and said, "Billy Joe came by today."

Gerald's head jerked around. "He what?"

"He came by to apologize and offer to help around the house. He said his mama set him straight. So he's trying to do right." I handed the business card to Gerald.

He turned the card forward and back in his hand as he sipped his coffee. "Well, it's about damn time he stands up and flies right."

"Do you think he can be trusted?"

Gerald took his cap off and ran his hand through what little hair he had and back down across his face.

"To be honest, I'm not sure. Maybe some outside work would be okay?"

"That's kind of what I was thinking," I said. "But I was also thinking Hank may have hired him to get close to me again to see if there is really hidden treasure here."

"That's always a possibility. I see you put some locks and latches up."

"Do you think I overdid it?"

He got up and looked around. "Well, you didn't have to put them on all the doors of the house. I was kind of thinking about the basement door and reinforcement of the front and back door." He looked at me with a grin.

I shrugged. "Better safe than sorry, right?"

Gerald chuckled. "Yeah, but the kitchen door into the hallway? Did you really have to put a latch here?"

"I put one on the bedroom and bathroom door, too." I laughed along with Gerald. It felt good to laugh again.

I knew in my heart it would never feel safe again in this house, and putting latches on all the doors would give me at least a little comfort. Of course, it didn't hurt having Gerald as a close and constant friend.

"Gerald, there is one more thing I want to mention. It may not mean anything, but you know how unusual this house is. I feel that maybe you can tell me if it means anything."

"What's on your mind, Cher?"

"I found this today in the fireplace outside." I dug out the piece of silver from my jacket pocket hanging on a coat stand and handed it to Gerald.

He turned it in his hand and said, "This is unusual looking. Where did you find it?"

"That night I was kidnapped, and I tried to get away, I grabbed at the bricks of the fireplace and one came out. Inside is where I found the key. It is a key, right?"

"Well, I've never seen one like this, but, yeah, I think so."

He handed the key back to me and I placed it in my pants pocket.

"You sure have had a busy day."

"Yeah, it's kind of weird; I've seen not only a crooked lawyer but also a thief just a day apart."

Gerald's eyebrow rose with a questioning look. "You know, that is kind of strange, that those two bozos would just happen by."

Gerald took one last gulp of coffee, placed the cup in the sink, and tapped the brim of his hat. "Gotta hit the road, Cher. I'll check on you tomorrow." I watched Gerald until he got to the door. "Don't forget to call me if you need me."

Before I could respond, he was already out the door. I walked over and locked up. As I was walking away, I could hear from a distance his car idling and some voices. I leaned over and peeked out the curtain. The sun was setting and darkness was descending quickly. I saw a person leaning down by Gerald's car at the end of the driveway. "Who could that be?" Curious to know who was talking to Gerald, I unlocked the door and looked out. There was no one there. They were already gone.

Confused, I slowly closed the door and started to latch the chain of the door when a tingling started at my neck and went down my back from a cool breeze behind me. Dread engulfed me as I cautiously turned around. At, the top of the stairs stood that old wheelchair from the attic. The shock hit me as my hand went to my chest. I tried to move, but I was already pinned up against the door.

My eyes widened as I saw the chair move to the edge of the landing, then down the stairs towards me. I screamed with everything I had, closing my eyes and bracing for the impact. Shivering in fear, I waited and waited. Cautiously, I opened my eyes to see nothing. I exhaled in relief and slumped back against the door. What was going on here? Did I really see old man Andrew's wheelchair? Was his ghost still here? After all, he did photo-bomb Aunt Pauline's picture.

Quickly, I double-checked the locks on the doors in the hallway and sat in Old Blue with a soft throw. What was the point of latching all the doors when there was no escape from the entity that lived within?

I couldn't understand why I had so many supernatural things happening in my life. First, it was an angel in New York, then there was Aunt Pauline, or was it my mom the whole time, and then Jessie's parents across the bayou and now a haunted wheelchair or even worse, an old French gangster who hung out with Bonnie and Clyde. I giggled. I wondered if Bonnie and Clyde were here, too. "Oh Lord, can we please go to another chapter in my life, one with no haunting." I took my last pain pill of the day and reclined my chair and was asleep in no time.

In the night, as I slept, I heard a slight movement in the room. My eyes opened in the darkness to see what looked like someone walking away from me. I was so groggy I could hardly keep my eyes open. Could that be... "Jessie, is that you?" I whispered.

Peeking through my eyelids, I saw the figure had turned to look at me. "Jessie!" As I was struggling to sit up the figure disappeared into the dark. "Jessie, please don't leave me." I tried to get up from the chair, but my legs felt like dead weight. They wouldn't move and I fell on the floor unable to move and fell into the dark shadows of sleep.

CHAPTER 26

The sound of birds outside roused me from sleep. I was on the couch covered with my soft, warm throw. Confusion hit my head like a rock. What was I doing on the couch? I went to sleep on the chair. "Jessie?" I sat up immediately and relived the previous night. Was that a nightmare? Was it real?

I shivered; it was so cold in the house. That's when I noticed the front door was wide open. Oh no, not again. Maybe that was Hank last night? Maybe it was those pain pills? No, it couldn't be. When I saw the chair at the top of the stairs, I wasn't on pain MEDs then. Was someone playing tricks on me, yet again?

Getting up, I pulled my throw tightly around my shoulders and walked to close the front door. How was it open anyway? I had locked everything up last night. Or had I? Maybe I got sidetracked after seeing the wheelchair.

After closing and locking the front door, I walked through the house. The basement was locked, but the kitchen wasn't. I investigated the kitchen but found nothing out of the ordinary. Searching some more, I found the bedroom door still latched, but the bathroom wasn't.

My hand vibrated uncontrollably as I turned the handle and walked into the bathroom. Nothing was out of place. Dazed by the dilemma, I walked towards the kitchen to make coffee when I heard someone knock on the front door, making my body jerk.

It surprised me to see a short, plump, older woman standing there instead of Gerald. "May I help you?" I asked.

She yanked on someone's arm on the side of her. "Did you offer to help this lady?"

"Yeah ma," the voice said.

I peeked to her side behind the front door frame and saw Billy Joe standing there.

"I just wanted to make sure my son came to apologize and to make amends to you. He is willing to help you out around here. Isn't that right?" she growled, looking at her son.

She turned and looked at me sternly. "I need him to work off what he did to you. He has to make things right. It's damn hard raising sons, you know."

"Uh, I've heard. Yes, he did offer, but…"

"Then get over there Billy Joe and pick up them limbs. When you finish that come sweep her porch and pull all that wild grass from around her house," she demanded.

Billy Joe was off the porch in a flash, doing her bidding.

"If you want things done right, you just have to supervise everything with these young kids," she said.

I was so caught off guard by her pushiness that I couldn't speak.

"We heard of all the troubles you been having and on top of everything else, my son had to make things worse."

"It's all right. He doesn't need to do anything around here."

"Don't be silly, missus. He has to know that if he does wrong, he has to make amends. I believe in fairness, don't you?"

"Yes, ma'am."

"Call me Dee."

"Okay, Dee."

"Now is that coffee I smell?" She asked, walking right past me into the house.

"No, I was just going to make some."

"Well now, didn't I come at the right time?" She started walking towards the kitchen like she owned the place.

I followed behind her, wondering if I should call Gerald. But what would I say? A pushy little old woman was making herself at home in my house.

"Lordy girl, it's cold in here." She went to the side window and opened it up. "Billy Joe, get some logs and come make us a fire."

"You don't have to do that," I insisted.

She ignored me and continued on into the kitchen, leaving me confused as to what to do. I watched as she pulled open one cabinet after another until she found the bag of coffee. She proceeded to fill the pot with water and make the brew.

I was dumbfounded at what to say. Should I get ugly with her and demand she and her son leave my property, or should I let her go ahead and get this out of her system? She obviously liked to do what she wanted and when she wanted.

She was little, but she sure packed a mighty punch, giving orders like a drill sergeant.

"Sit down, girl, while I get you some coffee. I should have brought you a casserole or a jambalaya while I was at it. I make a mean jambalaya; you know?"

I didn't think she wanted an answer, so I just obeyed and had a seat while she took over in my kitchen. Even though she had the coffee brewing, she was still opening every drawer and cabinet in the kitchen. What was she looking for now?

Once she closed the door to the pantry I had to ask, "What are you looking for?"

"Well, I was looking for some kind of pastry to go with the coffee. Hmm, how about I make you some toast?"

"That's okay, this is good enough."

"Don't be silly, girly, you are skin and bones. I'll make you some toast."

She continued to run from one spot to another, making toast and pulling out dishes. I wondered if anyone ever told her no.

In a matter of minutes, she had my coffee poured and was placing a plate piled high with buttered toast and jelly on the side.

I reached for a piece of toast and watched this plump, short figure of a woman with graying hair grab a broom and dustpan and continue to keep busy cleaning.

Taking a tiny bite of toast in slow motion, I watched her busy energy hypnotize me in a bewildered state of mind. I still couldn't help but wonder what this woman was really up to. Why is she here doing all this work?

"Yep, your place is really looking good," she said as she kept sweeping out the kitchen and down the hallway.

Something wasn't right with this situation. Nobody in their right mind pushes their way into a stranger's house and starts cleaning.

I stopped my overactive imagination and listened carefully. There was no noise. No sweeping or any movement. Quietly, I tiptoed into the hallway and saw no one. Where was that busybody at?

Tiptoeing down the hall, I looked in the living room, seeing it empty. I made my way towards the bathroom and then my bedroom. All my latches were unlocked. She had to be there.

Turning the handle and pushing the bedroom door, I heard a squeal from the rusty hinges. Put on my to-do list: oil hinges.

I heard a shuffle when I entered to see Dee sweeping around the bed. Looking closely, I saw the secret panel ajar.

"Hey, what's going on in here?" I demanded, looking at the gap in my wall.

"Oh, I believe in being thorough. I heard about your secret room and was going to clean it for you."

"Well, I believe you and your son have done enough. I want you to give me the broom and leave my house," I demanded as sternly as I could.

"Now, now girly, I've given up my day to come help you out, and this is the thanks I get," she scolded, walking up inches from my face like a standoff.

"Like I said at the beginning, you didn't have to do that."

"Well, now, we have us a dilemma." She walked over to the window and shouted, "Billy Joe, come here now."

I started backing up to exit the doorway when I saw her put her hand behind her back and pulled out a small handgun.

"Who are you?" I asked.

"Who I am is not important. What is important is that I get what is mine."

"Excuse me?" I asked, confused by her words and actions.

She pointed to the door and said, "Let's go sit down, shall we?"

"Dee, I'm not going anywhere until you tell me who you are and what you want."

"Well, for starters, my name is not Dee. It's Daisy."

About that time, Billy Joe came running into the bedroom.

"Get your brother, boy, and get me some rope."

"Uh... Daisy Wright?"

She looked at me in surprise. "Yes, how did you know?"

"You're the sister to the old man that lived here, Andrew St. Pierre?"

She gave an evil smile.

"You've been doing your homework," she said, pushing the gun into my ribs. "Let's go."

I walked towards the living room looking for a way to escape but knowing I could never outrun a bullet.

"Don't even think you're going to escape because I have you until I say. Do you understand me?"

"What exactly do you think is yours, anyway?"

"The money and jewels, of course."

"You can't be serious. That's just a rumor."

"I know my brother; and I know he hid out here so the French mafia wouldn't find him. I know for a fact he stole from them. I saw it myself. He made off with millions," she said with pride as if she had taken the money herself.

"So Hank was right. There really is treasure here?"

Daisy laughed. "That moron! He would have believed the sun spun actual gold if I had told him so."

"How did he get hooked up with you?"

Billy Joe came back in with rope and proceeded to tie me to Old Blue.

"Well, now, girly, that's none of your damn business," she said as she proceeded to open the closet and yell down into the cellar for someone named Wayne. I watched her remove the panel as the hairs on my neck stood up. In less than five minutes, my mouth fell to the floor. I couldn't believe who came out of the cellar.

"That… that's your son?" I asked as my body tensed up and tears gathered in the corners of my eyes.

For the first time, I felt a deep fear all the way down to my toes. Wayne was none other than the stinking, fat slob that kidnapped me and killed Jessie. These people meant business. If they would kill Jessie, then they would do anything. If there was actual cash involved, then my life was in jeopardy. There was no doubt these people were the lowest of the low and they would kill in a heartbeat for money.

CHAPTER 27

I sat there tied to Old Blue wondering what they were up to. I could hear rustling and banging in each room.

I had pulled and yanked so hard on the ropes I was sure I was bleeding. The pain in my broken arm was unbelievable. My thoughts went from the day I moved in until now. All the commotion and dishevel in this house were because of an old man's heist. So what? Did Andrew not share with his little sister and now she feels she deserves it?

Wayne, the kidnapper from days ago, walked up to me and slapped me across the face. "You little witch. Did you think you would get away with all the loot?"

"I don't believe that rumor. What makes you think there is still money here? Andrew could have spent it all."

From behind Wayne, I heard, "He led a very meager life here. There is no way he spent it all."

"So am I to understand he didn't share his wealth with you? That's what all this is about?"

"Of course, he didn't, that devious, stingy brother of mine. I followed him across America when I found out he stole the money. The money is here, I know it," she said, walking to the fireplace and inspecting it closely. "All you people had to do is just let me buy the house and we could have avoided all this mess."

"What? So it was you who wanted to buy this house when my Aunt was bidding for it." I asked. Suddenly it made sense. It must be Daisy that wants to buy it now, I thought. Was that sorry excuse for a lawyer behind all this, too?

"Yes, I thought, the only way to have the time to search this house thoroughly was to buy it. But since nobody seemed interested, I got my son Billy Joe and then Wayne to search your house while you were distracted." She chuckled.

"You mean distracted while being tied up underground."

An evil look came across her face. "Desperate times call for desperate measures."

I looked at the clock on the wall. It was still early morning, and it would be late afternoon before Gerald would pass by. Maybe someone in Gerald's department would see a strange car in my driveway and come to investigate. Was there even a car in the driveway? Or did they come on foot?

It shocked me to hear Daisy yelling at her sons. "I don't care if you have to tear this house apart one plank at a time, you find my money."

I wondered why I was left alive. I didn't even believe there was anything in this old house. Surely, I couldn't be of any value to them.

My body leaped when I heard pounding in one of the rooms upstairs. It sounded like they had a huge mallet tearing up some walls. Maybe I should have accepted the offer to sell the house when I had the chance, and then I wouldn't be in the middle of an armed robbery. But no, I just had to agree to stay here. Gee, the second armed robbery in one year. How lucky was that?

Oh Jessie, how I wish you were here. You would know what to do.

I watched as Billy Joe ran out the back door to return moments later with a chainsaw.

"What are you doing with that?"

Billy Joe glanced at me briefly but said nothing as he continued back upstairs. I listened as I heard what sounded like one drawer after another thrown to the floor in one of the rooms. After about an hour of continuous noise, Daisy walked out of my bedroom, her face red from anger.

She made long strides to me, then stopped when she noticed my jacket hanging on the coat rack. Billy Joe must have told her about the key. She turned it inside out then threw my jacket to the floor with force once she realized nothing was in my pockets.

Her eyes were piercing like daggers as she came and undid the ropes binding me. "Get up, girl," she demanded.

She started slapping my pants. "What do you have in there?"

I put my hand in my pocket and pulled out the unusual key and handed it to her.

"Well, now, what does this go to?"

"I don't know, I just found it."

"Don't lie to me, girl."

"I'm not. I just found it outside and don't know what it unlocks."

She threw it at me. "It must unlock a jewelry box or something."

"Ma!" someone yelled from upstairs.

She immediately ran upstairs, leaving me untied. I stuck the key back in my pocket and searched for a way of escape, but I was paralyzed with fear.

Out of the corner of my eye, I thought I noticed movement by the front door. My eyes widened in surprise as I watched the door slowly open.

Gerald peeked his head in the door, putting his finger to his lips for me not to make any sounds. Like a movie unfolding before me, I witnessed men dressed in black quickly and quietly surround the bottom floor. They each took positions waiting for the intruders to come downstairs. I noticed men in bullet-proof vests, not only local but also men from the FBI with their weapons drawn.

Daisy and her boys were making so much noise upstairs they had no idea my house was being invaded by police enforcement.

My breath was coming in short; quick bursts as I waited for the scene to unfold before me.

Still frozen in place, I saw Gerald motion me to go towards the kitchen. I positioned myself behind the kitchen door, peering out, getting a firsthand look of the action going down.

With everyone in place, Gerald slammed the front door, causing the noise upstairs to stop. Within seconds Daisy was coming down the stairs. When she saw Old Blue empty, she yelled to her sons. "Get down here, she's escaped," she screamed.

Everything unfolded quickly as they reached the bottom of the staircase where the police pounced on them, like gumbo on rice.

I couldn't believe my eyes. It was over. It was finally over. All the unrest of this old house was finally over.

CHAPTER 28

Slowly, I squeezed out the kitchen door to see Gerald wink at me and tip the brim of his cap. He puffed out his chest proudly and with a look of determination he helped escort the offenders out the door.

I stood motionless as one after another left the house, except for one small guy who turned to look up at me. It wasn't a guy at all. It was a female FBI agent.

She was a tiny little woman putting her gun back in its holster and snapping the gun in place.

I squinted my eyes as she walked towards me. There was something familiar about her.

She removed her cap, and her long hair fell down to her waist. Her hair was brown with graying by her temples.

My mouth fell open. "Aunt Pauline?"

She smiled, and I saw her resemblance to my mother.

"You can close your mouth now. Yes, I'm your Aunt Pauline."

"But, but you're supposed to be dead. Your tombstone is in the backyard."

Her eyes sparkled. "I have a lot to explain to you."

"Uh, yeah."

She reached out and took my hand in hers. "Let's go sit outside on the porch while I explain."

We both made ourselves comfortable on the front porch as she cleared her throat.

"I want to apologize for bringing you into this. But it was the only way for me to bring my dreams to fruition."

"Your dreams, what about mine? I lost everything that meant anything to me. Just to find out it was all a lie. You're supposed to be dead. So I guess this house isn't mine either," I said, my head falling to my chest as tears ran down my face.

"Please don't cry. I know I should have been honest with you about this sting operation, but I couldn't put you in jeopardy by knowing the truth."

"Are you kidding me? Do you realize the danger I have been in, like being stalked by a killer that held me underground and shot Jessie? Not to mention the fear I've been living in since I moved here?"

"I understand. I'm sorry you had to go through all that, but everything will work out perfectly, you'll see."

"No, my life is over without Jessie. But, if the house is mine, I want to sell it and with the money, I want to move back to New York. After all, I have nothing here anymore."

I watched Aunt Pauline's eyes cloud over as she tenderly spoke, "The house is yours if you want it. If you want to sell it, that's fine. But I'm telling you everything will work out. You'll see. The troubles in this old house are over. You can live in peace here if you want to," she said as she reached for my hand again.

I pulled away. "I can never forgive you for this."

"That's understandable, but I've been trying to close this case for many years. With your help and the help of the sheriff's department and my colleagues, this case is closed."

"What about that dead body in the cellar, or that stupid-looking dress in the hall closet? Well, the dress that used to be in the closet. Not to mention the ghost that looked like you and the water all over the floor in my room and in the hallway."

The corner of her lips lifted slightly. "The dead body in the basement was an unclaimed skeleton we used to make everyone think I was dead. Just in case they didn't believe, I just drowned in the swamps. With me gone and a young city girl moving in, well, we thought it would draw out the real treasure hunters. The ghost of me and water on the floor? Well, that's news to me. The only ghost here is Andrew St. Pierre."

"So you know about the ghost of old man Andrew?"

"Yeah, I caught him in one of my photos of the house. He never messed with me. So I never gave him much thought. Did you see him?"

"No, not him, but I see his wheelchair."

"You mean that antique piece of junk in the attic?"

"Yeah, that's the one."

"That's new to me, too."

"Aunt Pauline, how did y'all know Daisy and her sons were here?"

"We got eyes everywhere. You haven't been alone one minute that someone wasn't watching."

"Really?" I felt my heart open up to her. "You kept me safe even when I thought I wasn't?"

"You bet. I would never let anything happen to my beautiful niece. You must tell me more about that ghost who looks like me. But… right now I have a surprise for you."

I followed her glance to the edge of the driveway. It was Gerald.

"Why is he just sitting there?" I looked closer. "There is someone with him."

Someone got out of the car and started walking towards the house.

I stood up and walked to the edge of the porch. My heart started to beat faster as I slowly stepped one step at a time down the stairs. It can't be.

I turned to look at Aunt Pauline, who had a smile from ear to ear as she motioned me to go to him.

"Jessie? Is that you?" I whispered under my breath.

My feet seemed to have a mind of their own. They started off walking, then went to running as Jessie started running towards me.

I ran into his arms, almost knocking him down. "Jessie. Oh, Jessie," I cried as tears ran down my face like summer rain.

My heart exploded in my chest as I kiss him passionately. I grabbed his face in my hands and kissed him from his forehead all the way down his neck as he chuckled.

"I told you I would never leave you," he whispered into my hair.

I couldn't let him go. Jessie tried to push against me but only succeeded in moving me a couple of inches until he just let me be and he hugged me back as strong as I was hugging him. He then lifted me off the ground as I clung tightly to his neck.

Holding him around the waist, refusing to let him go we reached the porch, as Gerald joined us.

Gerald took his cap off and ran his hand over his head. "Man, I'm glad this is over." He looked down in thought, then up into Aunt Pauline's face. "Thanks for all your help."

"No, thank you. If you and Jessie hadn't been so diligent in your plan, we may never have caught them. I've been after these people for many years. But by killing off Jessie and leaving Sarah alone and vulnerable, it was just the bait to entice these people out of the woodwork."

"Yeah, that was a great plan and I'm glad it worked," Gerald said proudly.

"I'm just sorry we didn't find out where old man St. Pierre hid the treasure."

"So, you really believe there was a treasure?" I asked.

"Without a doubt," she paused. "He told me so himself. He said he would never let it leave his side for a minute. In fact, his exact words were, 'I'm practically sitting on it'," Aunt Pauline admitted.

It felt like a bomb went off in my head. "I think I know where the treasure is."

For a split second, everything stood still as I caught each person's attention.

"You can't be serious," Aunt Pauline said, her eyes bugging out of her head.

"It's in the wheelchair," I announced. "Why else would I be seeing it all the time?"

"That's good enough for me," Aunt Pauline said, rising from her chair. "Well, who's with me?"

We all left the porch and entered the house, up the stair and into the attic.

"Here it is," Jessie said, rolling it under the stained glass window.

I had only seen pictures of chairs like this before and since he was from France it definitely looked European.

Gerald and Jessie pulled on the corners of the seat cushion. I heard a tearing of fabric and underneath sat stacks of money. It looked like all hundreds.

As they turned the chair upside down I pointed. "Look under that straight piece. It's circular. Wait, I have a key." I dug in my pocket and pulled out the key I found outside in the bricks of the chimney.

I inserted the key. It fit perfectly. I turned it and took the small lid off. They leaned the chair over as Jessie cupped his hand under.

Out fell an array of gems, from diamonds, rubies, sapphires, and other jewels like I'd never seen before.

We all stood gawking at the magnificent sight before us. The light from the window hit each piece of jewels, making a sparkling fairyland in the room.

"I never would have believed it." I cleared my throat. "Does this mean we are rich?"

Aunt Pauline looked at me. "I'm sorry, but no. This is evidence as of now. But in time it's possible we can put this money to good use." She looked at Jessie and then me. "I guess you're not going back to New York now?"

I giggled shyly, "Not on your life."

CHAPTER 29

A peace fell over the house and land. The mystery was over and we could now go on with our lives.

As we prepared for bed, I asked, "Did Wayne really shoot you again?"

He pulled his tee-shirt off and I saw a small bandage on top his shoulder, just inches from his first gunshot wound.

"He only grazed me. I'm sorry we had to put you through all this. It hurt me to see you so distraught and vulnerable."

As I lay in Jessie's arms that night holding him close, I asked, "Were you watching me and keeping me safe, too?"

"With every breath," he whispered, kissing my forehead. "I hardly got any sleep. I was watching you like a hawk. It helped to know about the secret passageway and all the other hiding places. I was right under your nose the whole time."

"You mean you were here in the house?"

"I was never more than a few feet from you at all times."

"So I guess that was you I saw the other night. I thought I was dreaming."

He let out a low chuckle. "Yep, I picked you up off the floor. I said I would never leave you and I didn't. Now get some sleep."

"One more question. I thought you said that the fireplace was new."

"It is, well, at least half of it. The bottom was still in good shape so they just put new brick from about window height on up."

I thought it strange that the brick just came out with so little effort.

"I'm so happy you are back," I whispered, snuggling closer.

"Me too. You have no idea how hard it was to be so close to you and not able to touch you. But…"

"But what?"

"If something should ever happen to me, promise me you won't go crazy like you did this time."

"I didn't go crazy; I just couldn't move forward. My heart was heavy, like a boulder that wouldn't let me feel anything but hurt."

"I love you so much, Sarah."

"I knew I loved you, too, but I had no idea how much until now."

***

The next morning was like heaven. The rich aroma of steaming coffee being brought to me in bed like before, the awesome night being held all night by the man I loved. I didn't care if I ever saw any money from all the treasures. What I wanted was sitting right there before me drinking coffee.

A knock on the front door interrupted us. "Wow, Gerald is early today," I said, trying to blow more on the steaming hot liquid.

I heard Jessie invite someone in. As the voices got closer, I realized it was a female.

As they turned the corner into the bedroom I gasped. "Aunt Pauline, I was just getting up."

"Don't bother yourself. I just wanted to give you an update and hand you some mail from your mailbox."

"Would you like some coffee?" Jessie asked.

"No, I'm not here long. I just wanted to inform you we found some connections between Brian Thibodeaux and Daisy Wright. We got a search warrant and did a thorough search on his computer. We found enough material to jail him and keep him from ever practicing law again."

"Really? I knew it. I just knew it. Didn't I tell you he was crooked?" I said to Jessie.

"No, didn't I tell you?" We both laughed.

I looked at Aunt Pauline. "We both knew it. We just didn't know how to expose him."

I turned over the mail in my hand and noticed I had something from my lawyer. "Uh oh," I said.

"What is it?" Aunt Pauline asked with a worried look.

I read the cover letter and let out an enormous smile. "I am officially divorced."

Jessie took my cup and threw the mail to the floor, pulling me up in his arms. "Sarah, my love, will you marry me?"

I cocked my head sideways. "Well, maybe."

Jessie picked me up, kissing my face and neck and swinging me around and around. He put me down and kissed me long and hard.

I tried catching my breath, trying not to let my legs fold up under me. "Yes, I'll marry you."

"So when's the big day going to be?" Aunt Pauline asked with a smirk across her face.

I opened my mouth to speak, but Jessie chimed in. "The sooner the better. How about today?"

"Are you kidding me?" I said in shock.

"I've waited what seems like forever to have you be mine. I don't want to wait another minute," Jessie said with tears forming in his eyes.

"Well, it just so happens I'm an ordained minister," Aunt Pauline interrupted.

We gawked at her, then at each other. I nodded my head yes.

"Well, we need some witnesses, a permit and we can get married today."

"We have so much to do," I said, pacing the floor, then going to my closet. "What should I wear? Should I put my hair up or leave it down?" I mumbled out loud, oblivious to anyone in the room.

Jessie stopped me by grabbing my arm. "I don't care what you have on. I'd marry you dressed just the way you are if I could."

"Oh Jessie, my love," I said, caressing his face.

Aunt Pauline cleared her throat. "Well, you two get your stuff together and I'll be back this afternoon."

"We have to do it at sunset at my house across the bayou," Jessie announced.

"Okay, see you then."

In a matter of a few hours, we had everything ready and in order. We even had time to stop by Walmart and pick up some finger food, paper plates, and a bottle of wine for after.

Everything went so smoothly it was like the universe had paved the way.

By late afternoon we were all loaded in boats and making our way across the bayou.

The day was perfect. It was chilly, but not too cold, and the fall colors took on an awesome canvas of yellow, orange, brown, and green. My dress was a deep orange, form-fitting, V-neck, full-length affair with a matching lace jacket. Since I had been married before I knew white was out of the question so I wore fall colors. I left my hair down with just a hint of a curl to give it extra body.

Jessie was a stunning man, no matter what he wore. But the form-fitting red shirt and jeans were perfect for him.

Our witnesses were Gerald and his mother. She was so excited to be out of the nursing home for a field trip, which included a boat ride and some food other than her usual. She was having a good day and remembered Jessie and me from our visit.

As my Aunt and I set up the table on the dock and put out some food, I had to ask her again, about that gaudy dress. "So, why did you sew that dress with all the gems on it?"

She stopped and looked at me and giggled. "Honestly, I was bored out of my skull in that house and I love to sew, so I thought that maybe if I wore it around some that I could draw out the villains. After all, it looked like real jewels. I stopped coloring my hair and let it go white, then I walked around in public like I was in my nineties, hoping to mislead everyone into thinking I was a lonely old woman all alone in a house full of treasure. When that didn't work, then I thought of you. Of course, I had no idea you would hook up with the handyman." She gave me a wink. "That just made things harder. Don't get me wrong, I'm glad you had help, but you kind of messed up my plans." She paused. "You see, I knew what was going on with you in New York and I knew you would need a place to stay. That's when it hit me. A young, beautiful girl who knows nothing about this part of the country, alone in the house." She took a bite from a crackling then added, "I suspected Brian Thibodaux of his dealings with Daisy Wright so I hired him to contact you and to offer you the house, and to sweeten the pot I added a thousand-dollar monthly allowance."

"So it was your fault I couldn't find another job in New York?"

"Oh no, that was definitely because of your ex-husband. He had you banned from all advertising companies. I just gave you the option of Louisiana instead of New York working for a department store or something."

"Did you know about Hank and Brian?"

"No, again. I didn't know he intercepted your mail from Brian. Brian should have known not to give out your information," she said, sitting down. "The way I looked at it, Brian was using Hank to help find the treasure. He informed Hank about Billy Joe and once they would have found the loot, they would probably have kill Hank and take all the money and run."

I stood dumbfounded. So much had happened to me in the short period of time that I was in Louisiana and I still had questions. Like, were the angels aware of all this? Did they lead me here to catch these criminals or was it to meet Jessie? It's true, I could have stayed in New York working for minimum wage somewhere, but would I have learned about friendship and love if I had stayed? I just had to believe God had a plan for my life all along.

"Excuse me, ladies, but it's time. My parents are here," Jessie announced.

I watched my aunt slowly stand in awe of the sight of his parents on the dock. When I turned around, I saw Gerald and his mother, Geraldine, watching the magnificent sight.

Jessie took my hand in his as Aunt Pauline spoke her words of love and encouragement before man, spirit, and God.

When the ceremony was over, we looked at his parents, who were still watching us with smiles on their faces. Little did we know that that would be the last ghostly encounter we would ever have on the dock or in the old house.

When the party was over, and we said our goodbyes to everyone for the night, Jessie shut and locked the door. He then turned to me, grabbed me by my waist. "Now young lady, how about I do some renovation on you tonight?"

"Renovation?" I asked.

"Well, I renovated this old house to look new, so I was thinking I'd do some renovation on you and make you shine like this old house."

I giggled; turning every shade of red there was remembering him telling me this before. "Sir," I said. "You have my permission."

He grabbed me up from the floor, kissing me passionately as he carried me in his arms to the bedroom and closed the door.

ACKNOWLEDGMENT

This has been a very hard year (2020) with Covid-19 running wild along with the civil unrest in America. So during this pandemic, I want to acknowledge all the lives that have been lost not only because of the virus that attacks our body, but also the virus that seems to attack our mind causing much unhappiness in our country. May we put our differences aside and come together in peace and lend a helping hand to our neighbors and come together in love and prayer for each other and our world.

It seems God has called many people home this year. I have seen many posts of pain and suffering because of the loss of our loved ones. The world will never be the same without them.

May their light shine down on us from above with encouragement, and may they bask in the unconditional love in their new home as we reminisce about our times together. As you read this, acknowledge your friends and loved ones that have passed this year as I acknowledge mine, Barbara, Maruti, Eddie, Wayne, and Cecilia.

ALSO BY DONNA HANKINS
Louisiana Cajun Girl
Louisiana Bound
The Life and Love of a Chariot Racer
(Co-Author)

Web site: https://donnahankinsauthor.wordpress.com
Email address: louisianacajungirl1@yahoo.com

"Thanks for reading! If you enjoyed this book or found it useful I'd be very grateful if you'd post a short review. Your support really does make a difference and I read all the reviews personally. With your feedback, I can write better books in the future.

Thanks again for your support!"